RULE #2: YOU CAN'T CRUSH ON YOUR SWORN ENEMY

THE RULES OF LOVE BOOK 2

ANNE-MARIE MEYER

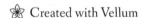

To my brother Daniel

CHAPTER ONE

For some reason, Principal Connell's office always smelled like over-buttered popcorn. I wasn't sure if he ate it or just preferred to use it as potpourri, but it coated the air with a greasy film. I shivered as I glanced around, trying to figure out where the offender was. Nothing. No left-over bag. No hidden microwave. The only thing I could conclude was there must be one of those warmers plugged in the wall emitting a heavy butter smell.

The office door opened and Principal Connell entered. He was carrying a clipboard with some papers. He'd lifted a few and was reading something. When he passed by my chair, he let the papers fall back down. "Good afternoon, Miss Hammond."

I tucked a curl behind my ear and nodded. I really wasn't sure why I was here. During sixth period, Mrs. Sauser came up to me with a note from the principal. It asked that I meet him at his office after school. He had a question for me.

I'm not a stranger to Principal Connell's office, but not for the typical reasons. While others come here to get reprimanded, I, as valedictorian, get asked to help out. I wondered what he had for me this time.

Principal Connell set the clipboard on his desk and pulled out his chair. Once he was sitting, he leaned forward on his elbows and steepled his fingers. "Thanks for coming," he said. His dark-blue eyes peered over at me through his thick spectacles. He had attempted to mask his receding hairline by growing his hair out and combing it over. If he'd just shave his head, he probably wouldn't look so old.

I nodded, shoving those thoughts from my head. Apparently, I spent way too much time here if I was analyzing Principal Connell's haircut. "What did you need?" I asked, shifting so I sat higher in my chair.

Principal Connell leaned back, his chair bouncing a few times. He looked contemplative. "I have a favor to ask."

"Okay."

Before he could continue, there was a short knock on his office door. Principal Connell leaned forward and called out, "Come in."

I turned to see the door open. All the air felt as if it were sucked from the room. Cade Kelley stood in the doorway. His backpack was slung over one shoulder and he leaned against the doorframe with the other.

What was he doing here? I looked back at Principal

Connell, who had an unsure grin on his face. "What's going on?" I asked, praying that my voice would come out normal.

"Come in, Mr. Kelley," Principal Connell said.

Cade hesitated for a moment before he sauntered—yes sauntered—into the room and plopped down on the chair next to me. He leaned closer and smiled. "Hey, Chocolate Milk," he said.

Fury rose up in my gut. There were a few things I never did. I never got lower than an A on my assignments. I never lost a cross-country race. And I *never* talked to Cade Kelley.

"I think this is a mistake," I said, grabbing my backpack and moving to leave. "I should go. I don't want to be late for practice." I reached out to grab the door handle when Principal Connell cleared his throat.

"Penny, can you sit down?"

My inner conflict grew. I was torn between leaving the room, where Cade was sucking the joy out of the air, and staying because the principal asked me to. My desire to please won out.

Principal Connell nodded toward the seat I had just vacated. I walked back—this time much slower. When I got to the chair, I sat. My back was rigid, and my muscles twitched. As soon as he gave the signal, I'd be out of here.

"Now, I know there's been some issues between you two in the past," he said, nodding between us.

Issues. That was a funny way of putting it. Issues were for civilized people. What Cade did to me all through junior high was just mean. Once, during lunch, I laughed so hard chocolate milk came squirting out of my nose. Lucky for me, Cade had been only a table away.

Ever since then, everyone in our class called me chocolate milk. It wasn't until Loni Patterson peed her pants at the ninth-grade carnival that my humiliation was finally overshadowed. But every time I was around Cade, he still brought it up.

I snorted and folded my arms. That was as long as I liked to think about Cade. If I dwelled on it too much, I just got angry. And Cade Kelley didn't deserve to have that kind of power over me. I wasn't going to let him.

Principal Connell shot me a look and continued. "I'm hoping that we can put those differences aside and work together."

"Work together?" I glanced between the two of them. "On what?"

Cade leaned back in his chair and sighed.

"Principal Connell?"

"Mr. Kelley has had some issues that were taken to court. One of the stipulations was that he remain at school and get some assistance with grades and fitting in. When the judge asked me who I thought would be best at that, your name came to mind." Principal Connell nodded in my direction.

Me? He wanted me to babysit Cade? I shook my head. I had to have heard him wrong. "I'm sorry, what?"

Principal Connell rubbed his temples. "I need you to mentor Cade. Just for a few months. Hopefully, with your help, he can get his grades up and get accepted to a good school. And, thus, avoid some unfortunate consequences for his actions." He narrowed his eyes as he studied Cade.

"Why are you punishing me?"

Principal Connell glanced over at me. "This isn't a punishment. Think of it as an opportunity. It even comes with a judge's recommendation. Think of how that would look on your application." He gave me a weak smile.

I had to give it to Principal Connell. He knew how to speak my language. Getting into Harvard Law had always been my dream.

"But as with everything else in life, this is not a requirement. Solely a request. You can turn it down if you would like," he said.

"Can I turn it down?" Cade piped up.

Principal Connell shook his head. "That is not an option for you."

I sat back and studied the floor. What was I going to do? On the one hand, it sounded amazing to have a judge write a recommendation, and that just might be the thing I needed to push my college application over the top.

But, it required me to spend time with Cade. Nothing was worth that.

I turned my attention back to Principal Connell. "Can I think about it?"

Principal Connell narrowed his eyes and then nodded. "Yes. Let me know tomorrow. If you decide against it, I'll have to ask someone else."

"I can do that."

Principal Connell smiled. "Until tomorrow then." He nodded toward the door and began rifling through papers on his desk.

Relieved that this conversation was over, I stood and slipped on my backpack. Cade seemed to have the same idea—we both ended up at the door at the same time. He glanced over at me and shot me his annoyingly cocky smile.

He reached out and opened the door. After a big flourishing bow, he said, "After you, m'lady."

I glared at him and walked out. Did I want him opening the door for me? No. But I also wanted to get as far away from him as possible.

Once I was out in the hall, I started toward my locker. When I heard footsteps behind me, I turned. Cade was following me.

I narrowed my eyes. "What are you doing?"

He glanced down at me and smiled again. What was with him? "You don't own this hallway; you do realize that, right?" He pushed his hands through his dark wavy hair. His bright blue eyes sparkled with amusement. Why did he take so much joy in torturing me?

I sighed. "Of course I understand that I don't own the hallway. But I know that your locker is in that direction." I stopped and waved toward the other hallway.

An incredulous look passed over his face. "Are you stalking me, Chocolate Milk?"

Heat rose up my spine as I sputtered. "I am not stalking

you. In fact, you are the last person I would even care about." I pinched my lips together as his eyebrows rose.

I hadn't meant to say all of those things. I guess pent-up frustration had a way of exploding out of me eventually. "I'm sorry," I said. I wasn't a mean person—he was. But every time I was around him, I just overreacted.

He shook his head. "Well, I'm happy you got that out of your system. Come on, Chocolate Milk, tell me how you really feel."

I let out an exasperated sigh and turned. I was finished with him. There was no way he and I were going to be able to work together. We were like oil and water. "I have to go," I said and stomped off down the hall. My day had been so relaxed, and now, thanks to Principal Connell, I was incredibly agitated.

I could hear Cade's laugh as I made my retreat.

"See you tomorrow, Chocolate Milk," he called after me.

I fought the urge to respond. Instead, I turned the corner and headed to my locker. After all my books were put back and the ones I needed for homework were in my backpack, I slammed the door and yelped.

Crista, my best friend since kindergarten, was leaning against the nearby locker with earbuds in, bobbing her head. I shot her an annoyed look, and she pulled her earbuds out. "What's with you?" she asked, snapping her gum.

I heaved my backpack onto my shoulder and started down the hall. "Principal Connell."

Crista followed after me. "What? I thought he was like your best friend or something. Did you guys have a spat?"

I glared at her. Her blue hair was pulled back into a ponytail revealing the under portion that was shaved. She had earring spacers and a nose ring. I loved her quirky style, but it clashed against my smooth brown hair and modest make-up. Mom would kill me if I wore anything but knee length dresses or jeans.

Crista's midriff tank top and miniskirt was a source of contention between me and Mom. Thankfully, Mom know that Crista was a good person, so she allowed me to hang out with her.

"He wants me to mentor Cade," I said as we turned the corner and headed toward the locker rooms. I was late for cross-country—I hated being late.

Crista sucked in her breath. "What? Wow."

If anyone understood my pain when it came to Cade Kelley, it was Crista. She had been right there with me during the chocolate milk episode.

I shot her a knowing look. "He says it's a favor. That I might get a recommendation from a judge if I go through with it." Even saying the words sent an excited jolt through my body.

A knowing look passed over Crista's face. "So you're going to do it then."

I shrugged, pulling open the locker room door. "I don't know," I said, leaning against the metal doorframe.

Crista snorted. "I know you all too well, Penny. You're

going to do it because you are sickeningly sweet and crave approval." She shot me a knowing look and slipped her earbuds into her ears.

I narrowed my eyes. What was so wrong with wanting the people in charge to like me? They were the ones to help me go places—to get accepted to a good school and finally leave this small Tennessee town. A place where once you landed, it was hard to leave.

"I do not," I said, but Crista was no longer listening to me.

She waved and headed in the direction of the art room. She'd hang out there while I practiced, and then we'd meet up together and she'd give me a ride home.

I sighed and slipped into the locker room. At least I was going to be able to work off some of my frustration. Maybe I'd finally beat my fastest time. Excitement rose up in my chest. I was ready to get lost in running and take my mind off Cade and Principal Connell's request.

CHAPTER TWO

"I don't understand what the question is. Of course you are going to do this," Mom said after dinner that evening. She stood up from the table and picked up her plate to bring it to the sink.

"Now hang on, Julie. It's Penny's decision," Dad said, raising his hand to silence Mom.

I stared at both of them. I'd thought that I could ask my parents and they would support my decision. So far, Mom had pretty much dictated that I would do it, and Dad was playing the opposite, wanting to talk everything through. Weigh the pros and cons.

Mom shot Dad an exasperated look as she rinsed off her plate. "It comes with a judge's recommendation. That's gold. And for what? All she has to do is help out some kid to raise his grades and social standing." Mom shot me a smile. "And from what I know about our little girl? She could do this in her sleep."

Dad grabbed another chunk of steak and set it on his plate. "But this is Cade we're talking about. The one that tortured Penny in junior high."

Mom shrugged. "That was so long ago. I'm sure he's moved on."

I wanted to laugh at Mom's naiveté. Sure, he'd moved on, we'll go with that thought. "It's okay, guys. I think I'm going to do it. After all, if it means a better chance at getting into Harvard, why not?"

After two hours of grueling cross-country practice, I'd come to the conclusion that I was going to help Cade. But I wasn't doing it to help him. I'd be a fool to think that I could just apply to Harvard and get in. I needed every advantage.

Mom shot me an approving look. "That's my girl," she said as she shut off the water and stacked the plate next to the sink.

Dad humphed and sat back, chewing his steak with a bit too much gusto. I reached over and patted his hand. "It's okay, Dad. I'll be fine."

He narrowed his eyes but didn't say anything more.

I felt bad for going against what he wanted. Today was the first time Dad had been home for dinner in a long time. He was always working late. I wanted to let him know that I took his feelings into consideration, just in case that became another reason for him to stay away.

"Do you guys even want to know how my day went?" Patricia, my older sister by eleven months, asked. She was sitting across from me, pushing her food around on her plate.

Mom returned to the table and sat, shooting Patricia a sympathetic look. "Of course, sweetheart. Tell us about your day."

Patricia smiled and straightened. She started talking about soccer practice, and I tuned her out. Instead, I thought about what I was going to say to Principal Connell tomorrow, and how I was going to feel now that I was forced to hang out with Cade.

Was he going to pull his dumb shenanigans like he'd done in the past? How was I going to change this ridiculous person into a functioning citizen of society?

Suddenly, the weight of my decision settled around me. The judge was going to write a letter of recommendation if I did well. Would he do the opposite if I failed? Worry rose in my chest, and I pushed away from the table.

I needed to know Cade's intentions before I accepted.

I brought my dish over to the sink and rinsed it off. After I set it on Mom's, I turned and excused myself. Mom and Dad were too engrossed in Patricia's story to notice that I'd left.

When I got to my room, I pulled my hair up into a pony-tail and checked my reflection in the mirror. I'd showered after cross-country and hadn't bothered to put on makeup. Should I?

Then I scolded myself. What was the matter with me? Makeup for Cade? Ugh.

I shook my head and made my way out into the hall, where I grabbed the van keys that were hanging on the wall.

"I'm gonna run an errand," I called into the dining room.

"Grab milk on your way back and be home by ten," Mom called back.

"Got it," I said as I pulled open the front door and stepped out into the September air. It was still sticky with the summer humidity. But by October, all of that would be gone. Replaced by chilly winds and the whispers of snow.

I bounded down the stairs and over to the van. I unlocked it and slipped onto the driver's seat. The car groaned as I started it up. Once the engine was running, I put it in reverse and pulled out of the driveway.

It frustrated me that I knew where Cade lived. I guess that was the curse of living in a small town. Ten minutes later, I pulled into Cade's driveway.

There was a single light on in the living room, but the rest of the house was dark. I turned off the engine and pulled the keys from the ignition. Suddenly, I wondered if this had been a bad idea. I really didn't know that much about Cade. How would he feel about me showing up to his house?

But I needed to know his intentions with this whole Operation Fix Cade thing. I needed to know that, if I accepted, he wouldn't screw me over. Like I was pretty sure he was planning on doing.

I took a deep breath and bolstered my confidence. I could do this. I was strong. I opened the car door and stepped out onto the driveway. It was cracked and crumbling. Now that I was closer to the grass, I noticed that it was in desperate need of trimming. The tips of the blades hit me mid-calf.

Kid toys and riding cars littered the yard. A sandbox sat in the far corner with trucks half-buried in it. It was such a stark difference from my immaculately kept house. My parents prided themselves on perfection. Everything was white and clean.

I headed up the walkway and onto the stoop. After a few knocks, the door creaked opened. A little kid with bright blond hair and big blue eyes peered up at me. He was wearing a pair of Mickey Mouse pajamas and carrying a toothbrush.

He grinned at me. "Who are you?" he asked.

I glanced behind him to see two more kids come up. Each slightly taller than the one before.

"Bryson, you shouldn't answer the door if you don't know who's there," a little girl with brown curly hair said, glancing down at the boy.

He ignored her as he shoved his toothbrush into his mouth.

The air grew silent, and I realized that everyone was staring at me. "I'm Penny. I'm looking for Cade."

The girl shook her head. "He's not here. I'm Olivia, his sister. I'm eight." She pointed to Bryson. "This is Bryson, he's four." And then she motioned to the other boy, who had shaggy blond hair. "This is Rex. He's six."

"Rex?" I asked.

She nodded, her curls bouncing. "Yeah. He's real name is Jayden, but his favorite dinosaur is a T-Rex."

"Oh." I glanced behind her. "So Cade isn't here?"

She shook her head. "No. He's working at the diner. Mom said he has to be back by eleven or she's grounding him." She folded her arms as if she loved saying that. Tattling. Such an eight-year-old thing to do.

I nodded. "Perfect. Thanks!" I said, calling over my shoulder.

All three kids watched me as I climbed back into my car and started it up. I waved at them through the windshield. Just as I pulled out of the driveway, a woman with light-blonde hair approached the kids and shooed them inside before shutting the front door.

I turned my attention to the road and headed north toward Tony's Diner, one of the only teenage hangouts in town. During the summer and fall it even had an outdoor dining option.

I pulled into the parking lot at eight. There were a few couples that were sitting at the picnic tables, and, from where I parked, I could see Cade standing next to a table full of kids from our school. The drop-outs and delinquents.

Of course.

His people.

I sighed as I turned off the engine and opened the door.

If I helped Cade, I was going to have to associate with his crowd. I wasn't sure I was ready for that.

I let out my breath and slammed the door. I shouldered my purse and made my way across the gravel toward an empty picnic table. I could hear the murmuring of conversations as I walked past. Secretly, I hoped that Cade would see me and come over.

After brushing the bench off with my hand, I slid onto it and waited. Five minutes passed and Cade didn't even acknowledge me. He stayed next to his posse, leaning against the neighboring table and laughing at something Buddha, the ringleader, had said.

I drummed my fingers on the table in front of me. My gaze kept slipping over to him. Finally, Tiffanii—yep, with two *i*'s—leaned over and whispered something to Cade. Suddenly, his gaze fell on me.

For some reason, I dropped my gaze and studied the table in front of me. Why was I embarrassed to be caught looking at him? It wasn't illegal. In fact, I had every right to. I was a paying customer. Well... I dug to the bottom of my purse and found a crumpled dollar bill and some quarters. I laid them out on the table in front of me.

Yes. I was a paying customer, and he was the server. It wasn't rocket science what he was supposed to do.

"Hey, Chocolate Milk."

Fury brewed in my stomach. I let out my breath slowly as I turned to meet his mocking gaze. Suddenly, all I wanted to do was stand up, march over to my car, and never come back. And never talk to Cade again. But for some reason, I also didn't want his friends—especially *Tiffanii*—to think that I was afraid of them.

So I forced a smile. "I've always avoided this place because I heard the service is somewhat lacking. Now I understand why." I narrowed my gaze.

Cade pressed his palm to his heart and faked pain. "Ouch, CM. Way to hit me where it hurts. My job performance." He stuck out his bottom lip. "What did I ever do to you?" He pretended to wipe away a tear.

I hesitated, wondering just how far I wanted to take this conversation, but then stopped. There was no use. "I'd like a hotdog," I said, pushing my odd change toward him.

He eyed the money. "Seriously? Things going bad on your side of town?" He took out a notepad from his back pocket and scribbled something on it.

I shook my head. True, my family lived on the wealthy side of town. But my parents wanted me to learn the value of a dollar, so they'd forced me to take jobs since I was a kid. "This was the change I found between my couch cushions."

I don't know why I said that. But I was tired of him always looking down at me because my parents had money. Like, for some reason, that made us different. Instead, it came out sounding conceited. Like the only money I could fathom spending here was my forgotten change.

"Well, I'm happy you finally put it to good use." He reached out and started flicking the coins into his other hand one by one. Once they were collected, he placed a dime in front of me. "It's $1.59." He turned and headed toward the window that lead into the kitchen, jingling the change in his hand as he walked.

I watched him go, trying to figure out something to say. A way to make up for being a total jerk. But he was gone before I could form the words.

Once he placed my order, he returned to his posse, leaving me alone to stare at the stained tabletop in front of me. Man, I felt so out of place. One, because this was not a normal restaurant for me to go to. And two, because I actually felt bad for what I'd said to him.

Since when did that happen?

CHAPTER THREE

After Cade dropped off my hotdog, he steered clear of me. I didn't blame him. So I spent the next fifteen minutes sitting at the table, picking off pieces of the hotdog bun and absent-mindedly putting them in my mouth.

His group of friends stood and said their goodbyes. I tried not to stare as they shot glances in my direction. Or when Tiffanii placed a very sloppy-looking kiss on Cade's mouth.

Bleh.

When I brought my gaze up to see what they were doing, I was met with Tiffanii's pissed-off expression. She'd decided to join me.

"Hey, Penelope. Nice to see you," she said. Even though her greeting sounded nice, it was slathered in sarcasm.

I forced a relaxed look and shrugged. "Hey, Tiffanii. Back at you." I winced at my ridiculous response. There was no need to give these people more ammo than they already had.

Tiffanii snorted and pushed her long blonde hair off her shoulder. "What are you doing here?" she asked, taking her gum from her mouth and sticking it to the leftover wrapping from my hotdog.

Well, that was gross. I crumpled the entire thing up. "I just wanted a hotdog." If she found out that I had come here to see Cade—I feared for my life. She had marked him as her territory at school. Cade was hers. Period.

She leaned closer. I could see her nose through my peripheral vision, but I kept my gaze forward. As long as I stayed quiet, I would be okay. She couldn't hurt me if I didn't give her any fuel.

"Tiff, they're leaving," Cade's voice piped up from behind me.

I saw her turn and then curse under her breath. When she turned back to look at me, she whispered, "Cade is mine and don't you forget that, freak."

Then she patted my back "Oh, my gosh, Penny. You are hilarious," she squealed as she stood and walked away. After a final, super-gross kiss with Cade, she disappeared.

My shoulders slumped as I tried to calm myself down. I was angry. I was hurt. And there was a part of me that was scared. Tiffanii got into a cat fight last year and pulled a chunk of hair from the other girl's head. She was crazy. And if that was the kind of person Cade hung out with, I was in trouble.

Probably too much trouble. I doubted that Tiffanii would understand why Cade and I needed to hang out together. She'd see it as me moving in on her man. Which was ridiculous. Cade was the last guy I would ever look at that way.

With his friends gone, Cade returned to work, walking around the tables and cleaning them off. I watched him as he gathered up the garbage and shoved it into a trash can.

For some reason, I didn't stand up and leave. There was something different about him when he was away from his friends. His cocky persona was down. And that intrigued me.

"Why are you staring at me, CM?" he asked.

That one little nickname snapped me from my trance. I grabbed the hotdog remains and my purse and stood. "This was a mistake," I said, throwing the garbage into the can and walking toward my van.

A hand surrounded my arm and stopped me. I turned to see Cade had weaved his way through the tables and caught up to me. He was smiling like stopping me was the funniest thing ever.

I pulled my arm up, breaking his contact. I hated how my skin burned from the absence of his touch. That was ridiculous. I *hated* Cade Kelley.

"So you want me to believe that you came all the way to my side of town for a stale hotdog?" he asked, folding his arms and leaning against a nearby picnic table.

The rational part of my brain told me to keep walking, get

into my van, and never look back. But he looked so relaxed and —as the irrational part of my brain would say—good looking.

His dark hair fell across his forehead, and a dimple emerged every time his lips tipped up into a half smile. It was like one of those bug zappers. I knew I shouldn't look at it, but I couldn't help it—it was drawing me in.

Suddenly remembering that he had asked me a question, I racked my brain for what it had been. But I kept coming up blank. So I straightened my purse on my shoulder and mustered a confident look.

"I'm sorry, what did you ask me?"

He quirked an eyebrow, and, for a moment, I thought he'd noticed me staring, but he didn't say anything about it. Instead, he said, "You were telling me why you came all the way to my side of town."

Right. The reason I was here. "I just..." I contemplated what I was supposed to say next. I wanted to ask his intentions with me, but then that sounded dumb. Like it was the 1800's and he was trying to date me or something.

Heat radiated my cheeks when I realized that I still hadn't answered him. What was the matter with me? I was president of the debate club last year, and yet I couldn't form a sentence for the life of me.

"Are you setting me up?" The words tumbled out. Perhaps, it had been the pressure of trying to come up with something to say to him.

He laughed. "What? With who?"

And then I realized how that question came across. "I didn't mean, are you setting me up with a guy, I meant, are you setting me up to make me look bad?"

His laughter died down as he studied me. Then he stood, grabbed the rag from behind him, and made his way over to the next table.

Why hadn't he answered me? Instead of finding his retreat as my opportunity to leave, I followed after him. There was a part of me that needed to know. Would he really stoop that low and set me up?

"Well?" I asked.

He glanced over his shoulder as he aggressively scrubbed at some congealed ice cream. "Seriously? You have to ask me that?"

There was a look in his eye that told me I'd hurt him. But why would Cade be upset that I thought he'd planned an elaborate prank just to make fun of me. Tiffanii was like that, and, from how close they were earlier, how was I supposed to believe that he was different?

"Really? Cade, you have to be joking." I glanced down at him as he scrubbed. "You've had it out for me since junior high. Apparently, I've done something to upset you, and you can't forgive me." I folded my arms. How had I become the bad person in this situation? He was the one who had relentlessly picked on me for years. I hadn't done anything to deserve it.

He straightened, which brought him inches from me.

His gaze met mine as he leaned down. "I was a kid, Pen," he said.

My heart pounded in my chest as he studied me. Since when did he smell so good? It was filling my lungs and making me all loopy. He held my gaze for a second longer before he stepped away and started wiping down another table.

Thankful for the distance between us, I let out my breath. What the heck had that been? Since when did I notice what a guy smelled like? Or the fact that they had gold flecks in their eyes? Something was seriously wrong with me.

Pushing aside all my weird reactions, I bolstered my confidence and approached him again. "What does that mean?" I asked.

He glanced up at me. "It means I was a kid. Geez, didn't you do stupid things in junior high?" He walked over to the soapy water bucket that was sitting on the windowsill and dipped his rag into it.

There were a lot of dumb things that I did in junior high, but that wasn't what we were talking about. "Yeah, well, I didn't relentlessly torment another person." I folded my arms, hoping that it made me seem more intimidating. But as the words left my lips, I wanted to pull them back. They came across as more accusatory than I wanted them to.

Cade widened his eyes. "Wow. I'm sorry. I didn't realize

that I'd hurt you that bad." He made his way over to another table.

Okay, so maybe he hadn't tortured me as much as I was making it out to be. Sure, he'd called me chocolate milk and got the whole soccer team to do it. But that was all.

I sank onto the bench and sighed. Why was I letting the past get me all worked up? Why was I letting Cade bother me? I was a success despite what he'd done to me.

"It's okay. I'm sorry for freaking out on you." I pushed a few grains of salt around on the table in front of me.

He glanced back at me with a smile on his lips. "Whoa. The great Penelope Hammond is apologizing to me?" He raised his hands to the sky and tipped his head back. "It's a miracle."

I bit my lip, trying to fight back the retort that lingered on the tip of my tongue. When he straightened, he eyed me as if he expected me to respond. When I didn't, he nodded and returned to the tabletop.

I brought my knees up onto the bench next to me. "So, when did you start dating Tiffanii?"

When Cade didn't respond, I glanced over at him. He was wiping the table in circles and seemed as if he were studying it a bit too hard. Was it wrong to ask? They'd just made out like Cade was going off to war. It was pretty obvious that if they weren't an item, they were close.

"Tiffanii has made up things in her mind that might not be real," he said, sitting down on the bench and pushing his hand through his hair.

I studied him. That was strange. "She certainly kisses you like she knows what you two are doing."

He brought his gaze up to meet mine. "Why do you care?"

Heat raced up my spine and into my cheeks. I was glad it was too dark for him to notice. I wasn't sure what it meant, and I certainly didn't want Cade trying to interpret it. He seemed like he wasn't going to torment me, but I still wasn't sure about him. I needed to keep my distance.

"I don't," I scoffed.

He narrowed his eyes and then sighed. "Tiffanii and I had a fling a few months ago. It didn't last long, and I broke it off. Apparently, she still wants something." He shrugged and stood.

"Wow." What was I supposed to say to that? I really wanted to say the age-old birds of a feather adage. But he was opening up to me, and joking about it felt wrong. So I just pinched my lips shut, hoping that nothing stupid would come out.

"So, you drove all the way down here to delve into my ex-girlfriends?" He peered up at me through his dark hair that had fallen in front of his eyes.

I cleared my throat in an attempt to push out the thought of how good he looked. That was not how I was supposed to see Cade. He was the ridiculous, mean boy from junior high.

I shook my head. "I guess I just wanted to know if you

were trying to set me up to fail, or if you really wanted to do whatever this judge wants you to do."

His expression turned hard and his jaw flexed. Had I said the wrong thing? I just held his gaze until his face relaxed and his normal cocky smile returned.

"Well, you're just going to have to trust me," he said as he turned and walked over to the window. He dropped his rag into the bucket and then pulled the whole thing off the shelf. He carried it over to the door on the side of the building. "We'll see you tomorrow, Chocolate Milk," he said as he disappeared inside. The slamming of the door marked his departure.

I stood in the middle of the eating area, alone. I took a deep breath and headed to the van. Once inside, I stared at the steering wheel. What had just happened?

CHAPTER FOUR

The evening's events played through my mind as I pulled out of the diner's parking lot. I tried to digest just what had happened, but I couldn't quite figure Cade out. I'd always thought he was some stuck-up kid with a bad attitude. But there had been moments when we were talking that had proved that conclusion false.

It was very unsettling to think you knew a person just to have them prove you wrong.

Just as I was a minute down the highway, my van sputtered and died. My heart leapt in my chest as I stared down at the dashboard. Out of gas?

I sighed as I rested my forehead on the steering wheel. How had I missed that? How had I gotten all the way to the diner without noticing that the gauge was on empty?

I reached over to my purse and grabbed out my phone. It was 9:30. I had a half hour before I needed to be home. After I found *Home* in my contacts, I hit talk.

Ten rings later and the answering machine picked up. Where was everyone? I tried one more time, but no one answered. My parents were old school and still had a landline. They both had cellphones, but, in an effort to reconnect or something, they'd both given them up for the week. The timing couldn't have been more perfect.

I found Patricia's name and called her.

She answered on the second ring. "What do you want?" she asked.

I gritted my teeth. Patricia and I didn't get along. I tried, but she was just so harsh. It was hard to always be the positive person in the relationship. So I just steered clear of her.

"Hey, I ran out of gas. Where's Mom and Dad?"

She scoffed. "How should I know. I'm at Brent's."

I tried not to roll my eyes. Brent, Patricia's boyfriend, was the worst. He was total Emo with black hair and black fingernails. I think Mom and Dad felt bad for all the attention they've given me, so they allow Patricia to date a guy who looks like he walked out of a Day of the Dead poster.

And he was weird. Like, when he talks, he gives me goosebumps. Not the good ones. The ones that tell you a serial killer is in your attic.

"Well, I tried calling the house, and they didn't answer." I kind of wanted Patricia to offer to help me. It felt strange asking her.

"I'm sure a gas station isn't too far. Just walk."

I scoffed. Seriously? I was her sister. She couldn't pull herself away from her boyfriend long enough to come help me? "Fine. I'll figure something out."

"I'm sure you will. Bye."

Before I could respond, she hung up the phone.

Now alone, the only thing that filled the silence was the occasional car that whipped by me. I shoved my phone back into my purse and headed back toward the on ramp. Hopefully there was a gas station not too far down the road.

Fifteen minutes later, I was still walking and hadn't found any place that sold gas. Curse of living in a small town—there was too much space. Which hadn't really bothered me until I was forced to walk it. Now, it just seemed ridiculous.

The roaring of a motorcycle filled my ears as it raced past me. I moved closer to the field that lined the road. I did not want to get hit by some idiot who thought they were invincible.

I hesitated as the sound of the motorcycle slowed and then grew louder again. Were they coming back toward me? Why? Darkness had filled the sky, and the only light was from the slivered moon. I reached into my purse as I heard the motorcycle creep up behind me and idle. My fingers felt for my mace.

This was it. This was how I was going to die.

The crunch of gravel sounded behind me as whoever it was climbed off the bike and made their way toward me. I rested my finger on the trigger and counted down.

"Chocolate Milk?"

But before it registered who it was, I had turned and readied my spray. Luckily, I recognized Cade's surprised eyes before I pressed down on the trigger. He raised his hands in front of his face.

Feeling like an idiot, I lowered the spray. "What's the matter with you? Creeping up on me like that." I locked the trigger and slipped the mace back into my purse.

"I thought you knew it was me," he said, keeping his hands up and peering over at me.

I glanced behind him to see his motorcycle propped up. "Since when did you get a bike?" I asked, nodding toward it.

"This summer. I think it's my mom's way of saying she was sorry or something." He pinched his lips together—he hadn't meant to say that.

"Sorry? For what?"

He shook his head. "Never mind. Let's focus on you. Why are you walking down the highway?"

I rubbed my neck. Tension was building up in it. "Shows how much you know about me. This is my favorite activity. I call it walking in the moonlight and trying not to get killed." I shot him a smirk. "You should try it sometime."

He rolled his eyes. "Where's your van?"

I pointed down the road. I couldn't see it anymore.

He followed my gesture and then turned back to me. "Wanna ride?"

"On that?" I asked, nodding toward his bike.

He nodded. "It's safe."

I laughed. "Right. I'd rather walk across the busy highway blindfolded." He quirked an eyebrow, and I sighed. "Okay, that's a bit dramatic, but I'm not getting on that."

He looked at me and then shrugged. "Suit yourself," he said as he turned and threw his keys into the air.

I watched as he walked over and put his helmet back on. For some reason, I was shocked that he was just leaving me here. But that was stupid. I had just told him I didn't want a ride.

"Hang on," I said as I walked over to meet him.

He glanced back at me. "Change your mind?"

I eyed the motorcycle. "Do you have a helmet?"

He reached behind the bike and emerged with one in hand. "It's for all the girls I take out."

He winked at me, and I knew that I shouldn't react to it, but I did. Heat pricked my neck. I cleared my throat and shook my head. I was acting crazy. I needed to get home, go to bed, and forget everything that had happened.

His expression softened. "Seriously, though? I have it for saving girls from walking down the highway."

I rolled my eyes as I took the helmet. "Yeah, you're a real knight in shining armor. I just need a ride to the gas station and then back to my van. Simple."

He nodded and swung his leg over the bike. He pulled the handles straight and flipped the kickstand up. He looked at me expectantly.

Right. I was going to have to climb onto the bike behind him. I really hadn't thought this through. I didn't like how close I was going to have to be to him. And the fact that I might have to wrap my arms around him? Yeah, not what I wanted to do.

But I forced out all my doubts and climbed on behind him. The seat was tipped forward, which meant I tipped forward. My hips pressed against his. I swallowed as I kept my hands at my side. There was no way I was putting myself even closer to him.

"You're going to have to wrap your arms around me, CM," he called back.

I shook my head and closed my eyes, grateful that he couldn't see how nervous this made me. "I'm okay," I called back.

He turned so he could study me and then shrugged. "Suit yourself. You're going to go flying off." He started the motorcycle and it roared to life. A few seconds later, we took off down the road, and I screamed.

Terror filled my body as I was whipped back. Desperate to save myself, I wrapped my arms around his chest and closed my eyes. I could feel his laugh rumble in his chest. Great. Just another thing for him to make fun of me about.

I'd graduated from Chocolate Milk to Screamer.

A few minutes into the ride, I began to settle down. I loosened my grip on him from certain death to fearing for your life. With my grasp loosened, I noticed just how good he felt. His chest and back were broad and...muscular?

What was the matter with me? This was my enemy. My sworn nemesis. I wasn't supposed to be riding behind him on a motorcycle, reveling in the feeling of his abs and pecs. Something seriously weird was happening to me.

But I was too scared to let go, so I forced myself to think of anything but how good Cade's body felt. I closed my eyes and started reviewing my notes for my Chemistry exam. When the motorcycle slowed, I sighed, relieved that this was almost over.

He pulled into the gas station and stopped at a pump. As soon as the kickstand was down, I was off. My legs hurt from riding, but I forced them to carry me a few feet away. I needed space from Cade before I said or did something stupid.

"You're going to need to buy a can," he said, nodding toward the convenience store. I tried to ignore the smug smile on his lips. There was no way he'd enjoyed that, was there?

Instead of dissecting his reaction, I nodded and stumbled inside. After finding the can and buying it, I walked back outside. Cade was leaning against his bike with his arms folded. His dark hair was swept across his forehead, and his eyes stared off into the distance.

I allowed myself to think, for a single second, that he was really good looking. I think I never saw it before because I'd been so focused on hating him. But right now, seeing him standing there, I had to admit, he was hot.

And then he looked at me and caught me staring. I dropped my gaze and picked up my pace. I needed to get out of here.

"You okay?" he asked with a hint of teasing in his voice.

I nodded as I set the can down next to the pump and swiped my card. "Yeah. Um-hum," I said as I pushed in my code and it was approved.

"I've just caught you staring a few times," he said. His voice grew louder as he leaned closer to me.

"You wish." I snorted and then pursed my lips. *Stop talking, Penny.* I sighed. "I'm just tired. You know, that dazed look. Nothing to do with you." I shook my head as I set the nozzle in the can and started to fill it.

"Umm," he said.

I glanced over at him. He looked as if he weren't buying what I was saying. But I was too afraid that I might reveal more than I wanted to, so I focused back on the can.

Once it was full, I replaced the nozzle and screwed the cap on tight. Then I straightened and shot him a smile, hoping to remove the awkwardness that surrounded me.

"All done."

He nodded and climbed onto his motorcycle. "Ready?" he asked.

I replaced the helmet and situated myself behind him. This time, it was more tricky. I held the can with one hand, propping it up on my leg, and wrapped the other arm around his waist. He started the engine and peeled off, more slowly this time.

It felt like an eternity before my van came into view. I was ready to unwrap myself from Cade and go home, where I would take a shower and hope that a good night's sleep would remove all of these conflicting feelings that had bubbled up.

After my tank was filled and the gas can deposited in the trunk, I turned to see Cade leaning against my van, watching me. There was a look in his eyes that made me blush and feel angry at the same time. Wow. My emotions were out of whack.

I brushed my hands against each other in an exaggerated movement. And then I felt like an idiot. For self-preservation, I needed to get as far away from Cade as I could. At least, until I got a better hold on my crazy emotions.

"Thanks," I said, pushing the loose strands of hair out of my face and tucking them behind my ear. Why did I suddenly feel so nervous around Cade?

He glanced over at me and smiled. Like, a genuine smile. I was a bit taken back by it. I didn't know that he could do something like that.

"Of course," he said, pushing off the van and stepping closer to me.

My heart hammered in my chest. My breathing changed. The thought that I was having a heart attack flitted through my mind. When he met my gaze, he grew serious. "Anything for you"—he leaned toward me—"Chocolate Milk."

The foggy haze that had clouded my vision parted, and his cocky smile was back. I groaned and pushed past him; the sound of his chuckle filled the air. I pulled open the driver's door and slammed it. Once the engine was started, I peeled out onto the freeway. When I glanced in the rearview mirror, I saw that he'd climbed onto his motorcycle and was securing his helmet.

I tightened my grip on the steering wheel and drove home. Whatever I had been feeling before was definitely gone. Cade Kelley was not my friend, and he most certainly was not whatever my hormones were trying to convince me he was.

CHAPTER FIVE

I dropped my lunchbox on the table beside Crista the next day. I had successfully avoided Cade all morning. Even though he was in my Ceramics and Calculus classes, I had kept my gaze down and focused on my schoolwork. Thankfully, Cade didn't seem eager to chat with me either.

I pulled out my chair, and its legs scraped on the cement floor. Crista glanced over at me and pulled her earbuds out.

"You okay?" she asked.

I shook my head and rested it on my arm. "I'm exhausted," I mumbled.

After I got home last night, I realized that I'd completely forgotten to write a paper for Economics. So I'd stayed up until five finishing it. One hour of sleep made for a barely functioning Penny.

"You gotta stop partying so late," she teased.

I raised my head to glare at her. "I wasn't partying.

Nothing about an Econ paper is a party." I straightened and grabbed my lunch. All I'd had time to pack was a semi-squishy apple and a roll. Well, now that I think about it, that was pretty much all there was to grab. When was the last time Mom went grocery shopping?

As I stared at the pathetic excuse for a meal, I decided that school lunch was better than this.

"I need different food," I said, pushing out my chair and walking over to the line. "Watch my stuff," I called over my shoulder.

Crista nodded.

Once in line, I allowed my thoughts to wander. First, they were about Chemistry, which I had next hour. But then they slowly morphed into Cade and what had happened last night. When I saw him this morning, he'd been hanging with Tiffanii, which helped kill some of the butterflies that had decided to fill my stomach at the sight of him.

But, even though I wanted to deny it, there was something there. And that scared me.

"You okay?" a voice asked from behind me.

I turned to see Jordan, the school's quarterback, studying me. My jaw dropped. Had Jordan really said something to me. Had he heard my in-distress groan and come to my rescue?

I forced a smile and nodded. "Yes. Thanks for asking."

He raised an eyebrow and then motioned behind me. "The line moved."

Red-hot embarrassment shot through me when I

glanced around to see that there was a good five feet between me and the girl in front of me. I turned and mumbled something to him and then closed the gap. As I grabbed a not-soggy apple in front of me, an arm appeared next to mine.

"That had to be real embarrassing."

I turned to see Cade with a smile on his lips, grabbing an apple and biting down on it. He winked and headed to the register. I stood there, like an idiot, watching as he was scolded by the cashier for eating something he hadn't paid for yet. He feigned a humble expression and paid.

Whenever I was in an embarrassing situation, why did the heavens feel like it would be a perfect time for Cade to show up?

"Are you okay?" Jordan asked me again.

I snapped my attention away from Cade, who had disappeared around the corner, and turned to glare at Jordan. He was standing next to me as if he expected me to move. "Geez, can't you just go around me?" I grabbed a granola bar and a yogurt and stomped over to the cashier.

Once I was back at the lunch table, I slumped down on the chair and bit into my apple. Crista turned to study me.

"Man, you look terrible," she said as she stabbed some of her salad.

I groaned and rubbed my temples. "Cade," I whispered.

She laughed. "What did the king of nicknames say to you?"

I shook my head. "I don't want to talk about it." And that

was the truth. What was I supposed to tell my best friend? That I had driven to his work last night to chew him out and then ended up having a very confusing interaction with him? That, when he wasn't around his friends, he was actually a nice guy and I wasn't sure how I felt about that?

Crista shrugged and turned back to her salad. I opened my yogurt and ate it. A full stomach definitely helped me feel better. I settled back in my chair.

I felt bad for snapping at my best friend, so I leaned toward her and bumped her shoulder. "Sorry. Hangry Penny reared her ugly head."

Crista shrugged. "Eh, I'm used to it."

Even though I knew that was probably true, it didn't excuse my behavior. "Still, I'm sorry." I sighed as I unwrapped my granola bar and took a bite. "I went to see Cade last night. You know, at Tony's Diner."

She glanced over at me. "Really? Why?"

"I was suspicious that he was just setting me up to fail. You know, the judge writes a recommendation if I do well—what is he going to do if I don't?" I took another bite.

Crista shook her head. "That's crazy talking. I'm sure the judge isn't going to base your recommendation on if you change Cade or not." She took a drink of her water and then chuckled as she set the bottle down on the table.

Embarrassment raced through me. That made sense. I should have talked to her yesterday before I irrationally decided to drive over and confront Cade. I pulled the rest of the granola bar from the wrapper. "That's it. You are going

to make all my decisions for me," I said through the chocolate and oats.

Crista studied me. "Why? What happened when you
talked to him?"

I pinched my lips shut and shook my head. "Nothing," I
said when she elbowed me.

"Really?"

I tucked some hair behind my ear and sighed. "Okay.
Some things happened. Like, he rescued me from the side of
the road 'cause Patricia didn't bother to tell me that the van
was on empty."

Crista raised an eyebrow. "Wow. That's...unexpected."

I nodded. "Right? Totally weird."

"Anything else happen?"

I shoved the remaining granola bar into my mouth and
shrugged. After I swallowed, I took out my books and set
them on the table. "It was the normal behavior mixed with
some moments where he was nice." Ugh, just saying the
words made me sound crazy.

"Nice? Cade?"

I couldn't tell if she was truly surprised or just mocking
me. "Yeah. It was weird and highly unsettling. I was
surprised."

Crista began to stack her garbage on her disposable salad
bowl—including my granola bar wrapper—and shrugged.
"I'm not. I've said it before, he likes you."

"Not that again," I groaned, a bitter taste filling my
mouth. The same thing happened every time she brought

her "theory" up. Something about how boys tease the girls they like. I never bought it. Mostly because I'm the exact opposite of the girls that Cade likes to date. He wouldn't be attracted to me. I was plain.

Crista glanced over at me as she stood. "Just saying," she said.

I flipped open my chemistry book and brushed the crisp, clean paper of my notebook. I needed to stop focusing on Cade and get these last few problems solved before class.

I couldn't let my grades slip because of him. I was stronger than that.

―――――――――

AFTER SCHOOL, I swung by Principal Connell's office and gave him my word that I would help turn Cade Kelley around. He thanked me and truly looked relieved. I wanted to ask who else he'd considered asking but decided against it. Now out in the hall, I turned on my phone and searched for Cade's number.

Kennedy High had an inclusion program that consisted of a school directory. That way, there was no excuse that you didn't know how to contact someone. It was strange, but I appreciated what they were trying to do.

Once I located his number, I hit the message icon.

Me: Hey, we are a go. Where do you want to meet?

I pressed the power button on my phone and the screen went to black. For a moment, the thought to wait and agonize over whether or not he was writing me back entered my mind. But, for my sanity, I resisted the urge.

My phone dinged a few seconds later. Faster than I'd expected.

I took a breath and turned my screen on.

Cade: Who is this, and how do I know you aren't a serial killer?

Ugh. Even his text messages sounded like him.

Me: This is Penny. You know that.

Cade: Penny... Hmm, don't know a Penny. I know a Chocolate Milk

This was going to be torture.

Me: I thought we'd moved on from all of that.

Cade: You may have. I have not.

I had half a mind to march back into Principal Connell's office and retract my earlier statement. Cade was hopeless. There was no way I could help him.

I must have waited too long to response, because he texted again.

Cade: It's a joke, Pen. Lighten up. I can meet you at The Jittery Bean at seven

I glanced at the time. That was actually perfect. I had time to get to cross country and then home for dinner. Mom and Dad couldn't get angry if I had to leave to tutor.

Me: Perfect. See you then

I slipped my phone into my pocket and headed toward the locker room

Two hours later, I left practice feeling refreshed. There

was something so nice about running off all of your frustration.

My wet hair hung down around me and shifted in the wind. I pulled it back into a braid as I walked to the Sienna. Once inside, I started the engine and pulled out of the parking lot. Two hours before my meeting with Cade. All the anxiety that I had worked off came flooding back to me.

Confusion filled my mind as I thought back to Crista and what she'd said. Could it be true that he liked me? Maybe back in junior high, but now? I snorted. Even thinking those thoughts made me feel like an idiot.

Nope. There was no way Cade Kelley felt anything for me. Ever.

I pulled into the driveway and turned off the engine. Grabbing my backpack and my cross-country clothes, I climbed out of the van. The screen door slammed behind me as I entered the kitchen. Everything was quiet. I dropped my backpack on the floor and hung the keys on their hook.

A quiet sob broke through the silence.

"Mom?" I called out, slipping off my shoes and walking into the dining room. No one was in there.

I entered the living room, I saw Mom wipe her nose with a tissue and pat her cheeks, like she was trying to hide the fact that she had just been crying.

"Hey, honey," she said, turning to smile at me.

I studied her bloodshot eyes and red nose. "What's wrong?"

Mom pulled a confused expression. "I'm not sure what you're talking about. I'm fine."

"Really? Then why are you crying?"

She stood, straightening her shirt. "Just stressed I guess."

I narrowed my eyes. "Mom..." I mustered my most unconvinced tone.

She dabbed at her eyes and smiled. I could tell it was forced. "I'm fine, Penny. I'm just overwhelmed at work. You know, sometimes you just need a good cry."

Even though I did know what that was like, I wasn't buying it. Things had been strained around our house and every time I tried to bring it up, Mom would write it off as emotions or stress.

Movement by the stairs drew my attention over. Dad appeared, carrying a small suitcase. His eyes widened when he saw me.

"Penny, what are you doing home already?"

Mom sniffed behind me. Something was going on. Was Dad leaving?

"Where are you going?" I asked, nodding toward his bag.

He glanced down. "I'm... I'm going on a work trip." He glanced up at me. He looked as if he hoped I would believe the lie. I didn't.

"Where's your work trip?" He owned a car dealership and had never been on a work trip before.

"Atlanta. They have a big car convention down there."

I eyed him. "Mom? That true?"

She scoffed. "Why would your father lie to you?" Mom would have sounded convincing if her voice hadn't broken halfway through.

I glanced back and forth between them. They were lying. But, if I were honest with myself, I really didn't want to know what the truth was. I just needed to leave. Get out of there.

Instead of answering them, I just turned and headed toward the kitchen, where I grabbed my backpack and keys. Right now, home was the last place I wanted to be.

CHAPTER SIX

I spent the next two hours driving around. I wasn't really sure where I was going, and the randomness of turning down side streets seemed to help calm me down.

Eventually, I ended up in the Jittery Bean parking lot, where I turned off the engine and grabbed my phone. There were still fifteen minutes before Cade and I were supposed to meet. I opened my Netflix app and picked a random show.

With the way my mind was swimming, there was no way I was going to focus on homework. Instead, some mindless dialogue with the occasional laugh track seemed like a better idea.

I got lost in the show, so when a hand knocked on my window, I jumped, throwing my phone into the passenger seat. I clutched my chest and glanced over to see Cade peering in.

I shook my head as I leaned over, grabbed my phone, and pulled on the door handle. "Geez, you almost gave me a heart attack."

He smirked back at me. "I didn't take you for a *Friends* fan," he said, nodding at my phone.

"I was just trying..." I let my voice trail off. There was no way I wanted Cade to know what I was trying to run from. That my parents just might be headed toward divorce. I didn't need to give him anymore ammo than he already had. I cleared my throat and shrugged. "What? Chandler is funny."

I grabbed my backpack and straightened. I needed to push out all the thoughts about my parents and how much it hurt to think that they were breaking up. I needed to focus. The last thing I wanted to do was start blubbering and crying while I was with Cade.

He eyed me as I stepped out of the van and shut the door. "You okay?" he asked.

I flipped my braid over my shoulder and nodded. "Yeah," I said, hoping it came across as nonchalant, even though it sounded squeaky and forced. I moved past him and over to the front door of the Jittery Bean.

"Okay," he said, but his tone told me otherwise. He knew something was up, and, if I knew Cade, he was going to sniff it out of me. He was like a bomb-smelling dog.

Once inside, the smell of coffee beans and scones filled my senses. I took a deep breath, ready for some caffeine goodness to make all my worries fade away. Or at least numb me from the pain that squeezed my chest.

I stepped up to the barista, who wore a name tag that said *Jessica*. She was standing in front of the register, with a peppy smile and curly blonde hair, which she kept flipping over her shoulder. "Welcome to the Jittery Bean, what can I get you?" she asked. Her voice was high-pitched, and I wondered if she had consumed one too many espressos.

"I'll get a short iced coffee." I dug around in my purse and pulled out my debit card.

"Of course." She tapped the computer screen in front of her and then turned back to me. "That's $5.37."

I handed over my card, which she took and swiped.

Cade was hanging back. His gaze kept making its way up to the board and then back down again. When he caught me staring, he shot me his half smile.

"Are you going to order?" I asked, taking my card and receipt from Jessica.

Cade shoved his hands into his front pockets and shrugged. "Nah, not a huge coffee drinker."

I studied him. "Then why suggest that we come here?"

He smiled over at me. Just then, the door behind the counter swung open and a girl with thick curly hair walked in. She glanced around the room, and when her gaze landed on Cade, her bright red lips tipped up into a smile. Bile rose in my throat as I took her in. Who was she? Had Cade brought me here to help him pick up a girl?

"Hey, Cade," she said.

I moved my gaze back and forth between them. Suddenly, I felt like I was interrupting something, and all I wanted to do was get out of there. Like, run out the door and never look back. But I felt frozen to the spot. This was a train wreck, and there was nothing I could do but stand there and watch it all go down.

Cade nodded toward her and smiled. It wasn't his normal, flirty smile. It was soft and sort of understanding. Which was weird for me to even think about.

She walked over just as Jessica moved away from the counter to start my drink. Mysterious Girl leaned her elbows on the counter as if she wanted to get closer to him. I really wasn't sure what was going on, but I knew whatever it was made me feel sick. And stupid. How the heck had I thought that Cade liked me? He was using me as a wingman to help him pick up chicks. I was so dumb.

I bit back the hurt as Jessica called my name and I went to the other end of the counter to get my drink. After picking it up, all I could think about was getting out of here. The last thing I wanted to do was stand there and watch these two make out. I turned and headed toward the empty table in the far corner—next to the guy who was playing some shooting game while he nursed a grande-sized drink. When I sat, I deliberately made sure that my back was to Cade.

After I set my iced coffee down, I unzipped my backpack and took out my Calculus homework, thankful I had that as a distraction. A few minutes later, Cade came into view. He was carrying a glass of water and looking pretty smug. When he settled down on the chair in front of me, he rested his elbows on the table.

I could feel his gaze on me, but I didn't want to look up. I didn't want to see what his plan had been in bringing me here or how effective it had been. Did she agree to go on a date with him? Were they planning on meeting after our session to make out behind the coffee shop?

Gah! Why was I even thinking about that? This was seriously the last thing I needed to have happen after what my parents were going through. But I should have known better. Cade wasn't good for me. In fact, every time I allowed myself to get close to him, I just got hurt. I needed to file that away in my mind in big neon letters that said CADE KELLEY WILL BREAK YOUR HEART.

Well, not anymore.

I forced a smile and nodded toward my Calculus book. "If you're finished flirting, please open your book to page 104, and we can get started," I said as I started to break down the next word problem.

He snorted. "Flirting? With who?"

I stared at him. Was he serious? "You've got to be kidding me." I leaned forward. "Why else would you bring me here?"

He quirked an eyebrow. I was almost convinced that he didn't know what I was talking about. Oh. He was good.

When he didn't respond right away, I glanced up to see that his gaze had not left my face. He was watching me with his arms folded and a contemplative look on his face.

And he looked good.

I stifled a groan as I dropped my gaze. Why did he have to look so amazing all the time? And why did I have to think that, all the time?

"Mr. Kelley? Can we just get this over with?" I tried again, keeping my focus on the words in front of me.

He chuckled as he leaned over and unzipped his backpack. "Always business with you isn't it." He set his books down in front of him with a thud. "I doubt you even know how to have fun."

I met his gaze as my lips parted and my jaw dropped. "I know how to have fun," I said.

He laughed. It was loud and genuine—and it made my blood boil.

After the evening I'd had, this was the last thing I needed. I didn't want to sit here and be mocked by the one guy I'd sworn never to get involved with. I grabbed my books and shoved them into my bag.

"Obviously, this was a huge mistake. I'm going to talk to Principal Connell tomorrow and have him get you another *life coach*," I said the last two words sarcastically. I doubted anyone would touch Cade with a ten-foot pole. He didn't care about his life or his future. This had been one horrible decision, and I was going to get as far away from him as possible.

"Pen, wait," he said, calling after me as I swung my backpack over my shoulder, grabbed my drink, and sprinted toward the door.

I needed to get out of this place. It felt as if the walls were closing in on me. Fresh air and the freedom of the outside world were all I could think about.

I kept my tears at bay as I pushed through the door and stepped outside. Seconds later, I was at my van and pulling open the driver's door. Right before I slammed it shut, an arm reached out to stop me.

"Penny, wait."

The earnestness in Cade's voice made me pause. It was involuntary, and I cursed myself for reacting that way. I kept my gaze forward, worried that if I looked at him, I'd break down.

"If this was just to humiliate me, I think you won," I said, my voice barely a whisper.

I could see him lean closer as he studied me. Like he was trying to figure out what I was talking about. How could he even pretend to be naive about what he was doing. I knew it and I was pretty sure he knew it.

"It was just kind of low. Especially today." I spun a keychain around and around. Anything to keep me distracted and help me push my emotions down deep, where they couldn't spill over.

"What are you talking about?" he asked. There was a hint of frustration in his voice.

I scoffed and looked over at him. His eyes were wide and the look of confusion on his face was almost laughable.

"Seriously?" I turned so I could face him head on. "Why did you bring me here? Did you need me as an excuse to pick up a girl?"

"Pick up...girl..." His drew his eyebrows together. "Does anything you say ever make sense? I came here to meet you. And I'm definitely not trying to pick you up."

"So the girl at the counter was what? A happy coincidence?"

The first look of recognition passed over his face.

"You mean Cora?" His teasing smile was back. "You thought I was using you to get to her?"

I folded my arms. For some reason, it felt as if my conclusion was slipping from my grasp. Had I read this all wrong? "Yeah," I said, but the confidence in my voice was gone.

He leaned against the inner door panel and studied me. "Wow. That really bothered you." He leaned closer to me and his cologne—or whatever he wore that made him smell delicious—wafted around me.

Abort. Abort.

How had I not thought this whole thing through? I got mad at him because he was flirting with another girl? This was not good. I forced a laugh. "It didn't bother me." But my racing heart and agitated emotions said otherwise.

He shook his head. "You can't fool me. You were really bothered by Cora." He pushed his hands through his hair as he winked at me.

He winked at me! This kid knew no bounds. Here I was,

sitting in my car, completely humiliated, and he winked at me. I needed to get out of here.

"I think I should go," I said as I started the engine. I was tired of playing this game with him.

He reached out and wrapped his hand around mine. I tried to ignore the zap of electricity that raced up my skin or how my heart doubled in speed. I attributed all of those reactions to how upset I was with him—not to the fact that he was touching me.

"Penny, I'm sorry," he said. For the first time, he sounded genuine. Like he meant it.

Braving the pain, I glanced over at him. His expression was serious as he peered back at me.

"There is nothing going on between Cora and I," he said.

Oh, he was good. I was beginning to believe him.

"Then why did we come here?"

He laughed, and I tried to ignore the fact that he was still holding my hand. Did it mean something? Did I want it to?

"I like the Jittery Bean," he said and then he peered over at me. "And maybe I heard you say something in Calc one time about how iced coffee is your favorite."

The butterflies were back and assaulting my stomach. "Oh." My gaze fell back to our entwined hands.

He pulled back as if he had been shocked by lightning. He pushed his hands through his hair, trying to play it off. "Cora is my half-sister. I was bringing her something from our dad. I figured that I could kill two birds with one stone." He shoved his hands into his front pockets and shrugged. "I had no idea that you would react this way."

Boy, did I feel stupid. Now I really wish I had ran away. At least then, I could live in a world where I was right and Cade was wrong. Now, it seemed as if I were this crazy, irrational person and Cade was the nice, sensible one. The considerate one.

My stomach sank. This wasn't good.

CHAPTER SEVEN

Now I felt stupid. Like, completely, totally, hide-my-face-and-never-come-out, stupid. And I needed to say something. Apologize. Ugh.

"I'm sorry," I said, staring at my hands in my lap. This was an interesting turn of events.

He chuckled. "It's okay. Completely wrong and illegal in all fifty states, but okay." He patted my shoulder, and I wasn't sure if it was meant to be supportive, but I took it as a bit condescending. But right now, I seemed to be misinterpreting everything he did, so what did I know?

"Yeah, but I could have asked instead of...freaking out." I glanced over at him and gave him a smile.

He studied my face before he shrugged. "It's fine." And then his flirty smile was back. "Should I be flattered that it totally bothered you?"

I rolled my eyes. There he was. The Cade we all knew.

"No. You shouldn't. Overreacting seems to be my forte right now." Especially since I stormed out on my parents just a few hours ago.

My gas tank was evidence of my unstable emotions. I had filled up yesterday, and, after my angry drive around town, I was already at half a tank.

"Wanna talk about it?"

I glanced over at him and took in his expression. It was almost genuine. Like, I could tell him what was going on in my life and he wouldn't use it against me. But that neon sign shone bright in my mind, and I shook my head. "Just normal school stuff."

For a moment, he looked as if he didn't believe me, but he didn't linger on it. Instead, he folded his arms. "So, what's the plan now? We can go back in there," he said, nodding toward the coffee shop.

I glanced at the doors we'd just come out of, but shook my head. There was no way I wanted to go in there. Not after I had made a complete fool of myself. "How about your house?"

His skin paled. "Probably not a good idea. My house is...busy."

I smiled, thinking of his little brothers and sister from the night before. They were so cute. When I glanced up at him, a pained expression passed over his face. Was he embarrassed by his family? Why?

Sure, his house was rundown and looked like it needed a good paint job, but his mom and siblings seemed nice. It may be crowded, but from where I stood, everyone seemed to love each other. It wasn't like my house, where everything seemed to be falling apart.

"Yours?" he asked.

I shook my head. Maybe a bit too soon and a bit too fast. "My parents are there, and they don't allow me to have boys over." As the last few words left my lips, heat raced to my cheeks, their meaning hovering around me.

When I glanced over at Cade, he was smiling. "Oh, and what did you think I was talking about?"

"I'm... Definitely not that," I stammered.

He feigned a look of confusion. "Definitely not what?"

Oh man, this conversation was sinking fast. "So, if not either of our houses, then where?"

Cade glanced around and then waved for me to get out. "Come on, I'll take you to a good place."

I hesitated but then climbed out of my van. With my backpack slung over my shoulder, I followed after him. He stopped at his motorcycle and handed me a helmet.

I was actually a little excited to ride on the back of his bike again. And it might have something to do with the fact that it meant I got to be close to Cade again.

As much as I wanted to tell myself that Cade was a bad guy, these last two days were telling me that I might be wrong. I mean, he saved me from the side of the road yesterday, and this whole coffee shop debacle had been entirely my fault. I'd assumed that Cade was using me when, in fact, he was trying to help me feel comfortable. He had thought he was being kind.

I was the irrational, freak-out person in this situation.

"Hey, Pen?" he asked, glancing behind him.

I snapped out of my thoughts and glanced up at him. "Yeah?"

"This only works if you get on the bike," he said, winking at me.

What used to be something I hated was slowly turning into something that I understood. Cade winked when he was teasing. I wondered if it was because he knew that sometimes his words could offend.

I wanted to ask why he just didn't say the offending things, but then I pushed that aside. That really wasn't something we had to get into tonight. So I smiled and climbed on behind him.

As soon as my arms slipped around his middle, my heart picked up speed. I could feel the warmth of his skin through his t-shirt. I could feel his hard muscles, causing feelings to rise up in my stomach.

Feelings that I wasn't sure I wanted there.

"You ready?" he asked. The tone of his voice had deepened.

I nodded against his shoulder, and he started his bike. Soon, we were cruising down the road. The wind was loud, which was nice. There was no need for awkward conversation. Instead, I just got to sit there, holding onto Cade.

And maybe, just maybe, I enjoyed holding onto him.

Because in this moment, we weren't Cade and Penelope, sworn enemies since junior high. We were just us. And I was beginning to like that.

CADE PULLED up next to one of the two water towers in town. When he killed the engine, I realized that this was where we were going to study. He pulled off his helmet and pushed down the kickstand.

I climbed off and loosened my helmet. "So this is your secret place?" I asked.

He grinned over at me as he took my helmet and set it next to his on the bike. "Have you ever been here?"

I ran my gaze up the ladder and to the little platform that surrounded the bottom of the tank. "Nope."

He grabbed my hand and pulled me toward the ladder. "Then you're in for a treat," he said, slinging both backpacks onto his shoulder and grabbing the bottom rung.

Soon, he was halfway to the top, and I was still standing at the bottom, staring up at him. I wasn't sure how I felt about climbing up the water tower. Wasn't this illegal?

That was the last thing an aspiring lawyer needed—a record.

"Is this legal?" I called up to him.

He glanced down at me. "Ah, come on, Chocolate Milk, live a little."

I snorted. "Wasn't living a little what got you in trouble in the first place?"

Silence surrounded us as he kept climbing. I couldn't tell, but I suspected that I might have hit a nerve with that statement. It wasn't like it was a secret that he had a run-in with the police. Principal Connell had told me. In front of him.

"Cade?" I asked, hoping that he wasn't mad at me.

"If you want to know, you should just ask me," he said as he climbed onto the platform and peered down at me.

I glanced up at him and then reached out and grabbed onto the rung just above me. It might have been his words, or the fact that I didn't want to be at the base of the tower by myself, but I pulled myself up.

It didn't take long before I was climbing onto the platform, where I met Cade's satisfied smile.

"And I thought you weren't an adventurous person. Look at that, you surprised me, CM."

As much as I didn't want to admit it, I kind of liked the fact that I had surprised Cade. That I actually did something out of character. But then the fear of getting caught and going to jail crept into my mind. "So, how illegal is this?" I asked, moving to sit next to him. He had both legs dangling over the side.

He glanced over at me. "I thought you were the legal expert. How would I know?"

I eyed him. Was he serious? "I figured you've had a lot of run-ins with the law."

He raised his eyebrows as he studied me.

I chewed my inner cheek. "I'm sorry."

"Whoa. The Great Penelope said sorry again?" He leaned toward me. "How much did that hurt?"

I shoved his shoulder, and he chuckled as he moved back. "I'm not as conceited as you make me out to be," I said.

"Wait. So you're saying my preconceived notions about you might not be right?" He dropped his jaw in an exaggerated movement. "Wha...?"

I groaned. "Are you ever serious, or is everything always a joke to you?" The words slipped from my mouth before I could stop them. I bit my lip as I glanced over at him. I felt like I should just record myself saying "I'm sorry" so I could play it back when I said something stupid. Which seemed to be happening a lot lately.

He shrugged and turned to rest his arms on the bottom rung of the railing. "I guess I've just known too many people who take life too seriously. I try not to." There was something in his voice that sent shivers down my spine.

I know I had asked him to be serious, but I wasn't sure that I liked honest Cade. He was intense. I sighed. "You're probably right. And I'm always serious, so it might be good if a bit of your come-what-may attitude rubs off on me." I copied him, resting my arms on the bottom rung of the railing.

"Wait. I can teach you something?" He clapped his hands. "Call a press conference and alert the media. Cade Kelley teaches Penelope Hammond a life lesson."

I rolled my eyes. Great. There seemed to be only two sides of Cade Kelley. Obnoxious or super serious. This was going to be a challenge.

"Okay, Mr. Bipolar. Let's get this Calc homework done before it gets too late and I get grounded." Plus, I wasn't sure how I felt about our conversations slowly becoming more and more intimate. This didn't bode well for me, and I was sure he felt the same. Keeping our relationship where it was at seemed like the best idea.

He grinned and pulled the backpacks closer to us. "Yes, ma'am."

After grabbing out our books, notebooks, and pencils, we settled in for a long night of Calculus.

CHAPTER EIGHT

The next day at lunch, I wasn't in as bad of a mood as I had been the day before. I think it had something to do with me and Cade and the fact that I had successfully avoided both of my parents since I'd seen Dad with his suitcase.

I didn't come home from our study session until ten, when everyone was already asleep. This morning, I stayed in bed until the last minute. I didn't even stick around the house for breakfast. I grabbed something on the way to school when I stopped for gas.

Now, the stale gas-station breakfast sandwich was gone, and I was hungry.

Crista glanced over at me. "You're in a good mood," she said, bopping her head to the beat. I could hear her music from the earbud she'd taken out so we could talk.

I sighed. I wasn't going to be in about a minute. I needed to tell her about what had happened with my parents the night before. Maybe she could give me a different opinion. Maybe what I thought was happening to my family, wasn't.

"Well, I think my parents are splitting."

She stopped moving to study me. After she pulled the other earbud out, she focused on me. "What? How?"

I sighed as I slumped back in my chair. "When I got home yesterday, I found my mom crying and my dad with a suitcase. They tried to play it off as a business trip, but come on, when was the last time my dad ever went on a trip for work?" I snorted. It was a ridiculous lie, and I was angry that my parents thought it would actually work. "Never."

"Oh, Pen. I'm so sorry. That stinks."

It felt good to talk about it. And Crista was awesome. Her parents split up a few years ago, so if anyone knew what I was going through, it was her.

"Yeah. Thanks." I sighed as I fiddled with the strap of my backpack. "I knew if anyone would understand, it would be you."

She patted my knee. "You'll get through this. I promise you."

I hoped so. I knew most of the kids at my school had parents that had split up, so it wasn't like it was a foreign concept. But, I guess I never thought it would happen to me. We'd always been the perfect family with the perfect house. It felt strange that it was crumbling down around me, and there was nothing I could do to stop it.

Crista drummed her fingers on the table. "You know what I'd do? I'd confront them. It's ridiculous that they are hiding from you like this. I'd call them on their crap and see what they do."

I smiled over at her. I'd always admired her bravery. She was a grab-life-by-the-horns kind of girl, and if you didn't like it, the door was right there. It was the exact opposite of me. My constant need to please people caused me headaches. Maybe I needed to take a page from her book. Take charge of my life.

"Yeah. I'll try it."

She studied me and then laughed. "You're not going to do that," she said as she picked up her soda and took a drink. "But it's cute that you think you will."

I chuckled, hoping to mask the hurt that bubbled up inside of me. It hurt that she doubted me. Like I was so wrapped up in other people that I couldn't stand up for myself. And even if that were true, I didn't need my best friend thinking it.

"Hey, I think I left my Chem homework in my locker. I should grab that before class." I gathered up my stuff and headed toward my locker before she could say anything.

Right now, I was an emotional wreck, and I didn't need to break down in front of her and the entire senior class. When I got to my locker, I sighed. What was happening to me? How was I losing control like this?

I pushed aside my feelings and focused on my combination. After I opened the door, I studied the contents. Truth was, there was no Chem homework. I'd finished that all last night. Like I was ever going to forget homework. That wasn't me.

After I gathered a few stray pieces of paper and threw them into the trash, I glanced at myself in the mirror and took a deep breath. I was only reacting like this because my emotions were all over the place. And there was some truth to Crista's words. I should confront my parents. I did deserve to know if they were getting a divorce. I just wasn't sure if I was strong enough to ask them myself.

"Oh man, one night of breaking into the city's water tower and you're becoming a habitual delinquent."

I froze as Cade's playful voice sounded from behind me. I glanced into my mirror to see him studying me with a half smile tugging on his lips. Even though it felt like he might be flirting with me, there was something he'd said that forced me to stop.

"So it *is* illegal to climb up a water tower like that," I said, whipping around to glare at him. "You had me break the law."

He laughed and leaned closer to me. I tried to ignore the fact that there were only inches between him and I.

"But it felt so good, didn't it?" he asked. His voice had turned husky, and I wasn't sure if he too was painfully aware of how close we were.

Breaking myself from the trance he had me in, I shook my head and turned back to my locker, hoping my warm cheeks didn't give me away. I took a deep breath, trying to calm my conflicting emotions.

"That's it. Next time we do something you recommend, I'm Googling it. At least a search engine won't try to coerce me into breaking the law." Not sure what to do, I fiddled with a few notebooks, shifting them around.

"Do I make you nervous, Chocolate Milk?"

I snorted and turned, slamming the locker door shut behind me. "Nervous? Why would you think that?" I stuck my hand out in front of him, praying that it wouldn't shake. "See? Not nervous."

Cade glanced down at my hand before he took it in his. "What about now?" he asked, inching closer to me.

Well, yeah, now my heart was galloping in my chest. I was pretty sure that Principal Connell could hear it from his office. I feared how my voice would sound, so I just shook my head.

After a few seconds to compose myself, I tried to focus on something else. "So, what are you doing here?" I asked.

He dropped my hand and pushed his hands through his hair. "Well, since it's Friday, I was wondering if you wanted to get together and study."

I eyed him. What kind question was that? Of course we were going to get together and study. "Do you have homework due on Monday?"

He nodded.

"And wouldn't it be beneficial to get it done?"

He nodded again.

I patted his shoulder, grateful for the fact that he looked a bit surprised at my touch. Maybe, just maybe, he wasn't as cool and collected as he seemed. "Then we are getting together." I shot him a smile and turned to head toward Chemistry. I'd just hang out there until the bell rang.

"Hang on," he said, grabbing my hand and halting my retreat.

It was becoming strange to me, how much he was touching me. Was it just his personality, or did it mean something more? I had only had an antagonistic relationship with him in the past, so these encounters would have seemed completely out of character. But now that we were sort of friends, I wasn't sure what this meant.

I was going to have to study him closer the next time we were around other people.

"What?" I asked, meeting his gaze. I hoped that he didn't see how his touch melted my insides like chocolate on a hot day.

"Since we are doing something you want to do tonight, I get to pick something for us to do after."

I eyed him. What did that mean? "Something I want to do?" I pulled my hand from his grasp and folded my arms.

He laughed. "Ah, come on. You can't tell me you don't enjoy any opportunity you can get to play teacher."

I stared at him. Is that really what he thought of me? That all I wanted to do was schoolwork? True, my life consisted mostly of doing homework, but I didn't like that he thought it was my hobby. "Well, Cade, you're about to learn so much more about me."

He whispered something like, "I hope so" under his

breath, but, by the time I glanced over at him, his lips were closed. He peered over at me and smiled. "How about I come pick you up tonight and we'll head over to the water tower to do some homework. My thing doesn't start till nine anyways."

I eyed him. I really wanted to ask him what his plans were for us. "So you're really not going to tell me what we're going to do?"

He pretended to grab a key out of the air and lock his lips. "My lips are sealed, madam," he said giving me a flourishing bow. "You will just have to wait and find out."

I glared at him, but that didn't seem to do anything. He just winked. It was obvious that he knew this was bothering me, and he seemed to enjoy that. I folded my arms. "Who says I'm gonna come with you, then? How do I know you're not going to take me to the woods and kill me?"

Truth was, I hated surprises. They always turned out terribly.

"Well, you'll just have to trust me," he said leaning in and wiggling his eyebrows.

Suddenly, I realized how close he was to me. I could smell him—feel him—and it made my heart pound. His expression softened as his gaze met mine, as if he too had realized that we were inches away from each other. Was it possible that he could be having a similar reaction?

He pulled back and shot me a smile. "Until this evening, then," he said.

All I could do was nod as I watched him wink and step

past me. He walked down the hall without looking back and disappeared around the corner. Just as I moved to head towards Chemistry I heard my name.

"Hey, Pen?" Cade asked.

"Yeah?" I turned to see him peeking around the corner.

"Try to wear something nice tonight."

I raised my eyebrows, wanting to ask more, but he just smiled and disappeared.

Wear something nice? Did he not think what I wore was nice? Granted, all I wore were T-shirts and jeans, but they weren't ripped or stained. And if we were just studying, what did it matter?

These questions raced through my mind as I walked to chemistry. By the time I opened the door, my stomach was in knots. I wished I could figure out what was going on. But from the look in his eye and his cocky smile, there was no way Cade was going to tell me.

When I slipped into my seat, I grabbed my phone from my backpack and pulled up Crista's phone number.

Me: I need your help

A few seconds later, Crista responded.

Crista: What's up? Did you find your chemistry homework?

The realization of how I had left our conversation at lunch washed over me. I felt guilty for lying to her. She'd only been trying to help, and I may have overreacted. That seemed to be my MO right now.

Me: Yeah. I did. I also ran in to Cade. After our study

session today, he wants to take me somewhere. He said to dress nice. Freaking out.

Crista: What does that mean?

I sent an emoji of a person shrugging their shoulders.

Crista: Haha. Well I'll come over after school, and we'll figure something out.

Relief washed over me as I texted "thanks" and then slipped my phone back into my backpack. Crista's style was spunky and cute, so I may not be dressed as nice as Cade wanted me to, but at least I would look better than I did right now. And for some reason, I had this deep desire to please him. I wanted him to think I looked nice because...

I shook my head. That was the last thing I needed to be thinking about. I had my outfit situation planned out. That was all that really mattered. If I delved too far into my thoughts, I'd turn into a walking mess. And no one needed that.

Thankfully Mr. Landon came walking in just as the bell rang. There was nothing like chemistry to keep my mind from wandering. At least that was my hope as he walked up to the whiteboard and started writing.

CHAPTER NINE

"It's pretty quiet around here," Crista said as we went up to my bedroom.

I glanced around and nodded. Truth was my house had been growing quiet over the last few months. I guess I hadn't really noticed until now how little people were actually home. Patricia was always over at her obnoxious boyfriend's house, and my parents? Who knew. It wasn't like they ever told me anything.

"Yeah. Everybody's got a busy life," I said, shutting my bedroom door and turning to her. The last thing I wanted was to talk about my family. Not when I had this evening to get through.

Crista walked over to my bed and dumped an armful of clothes onto my comforter. I eyed some of her choices as she began to separate them into piles.

"What did you bring me?" I asked as I stared at a leopard-print romper. Krista knew I wouldn't wear something like that.

"I know what you're thinking. But trust me, you're gonna look good." She turned and smiled at me. It wasn't one of those comforting and reassuring smiles. It was more like the ones the nurses give you right before they stick a needle in your arm.

"Should I be concerned that you're taking a little too much pleasure in this?" I took a step back and held up my hands.

Crista shrugged. "Maybe. But lest we forget, you were the one who asked me to help."

I laughed and nodded. "True. I'm a glutton for punishment." I sat on my fraying armchair in the corner of my room and held out my arms. "All right. I'm ready. Change me."

I should've gone with my instincts. Crista took way too much pleasure in doing my hair, makeup, and clothes. By the time she was finished, I was surprised I still had my sight and most of my hair. I didn't understand why she hadn't picked up on my constant wincing or shying away from her. Perhaps she had noticed—she just didn't care.

"Oh my goodness, Penny. You look amazing." Her gaze traveled up and down my body and a smile emerged. She looked like a pageant mom whose daughter has just taken the top crown.

I narrowed my eyes. "Should I be worried about you? Since when are you this into hair and makeup?"

"I don't know. I guess I've always seen your potential. Maybe it was a dream come true." She got a contemplative look on her face.

It was great to hear that my best friend constantly thought about what she could do to change me. It wasn't like we could all be Crista. She was the kind of girl who marched to her own drum. Sure, she had flawless skin, but she also had blue hair and thick eye makeup. I touched my face. What had I done? "I'm a little scared to look now."

She waved my concern away. "You look fantastic," she said. She grabbed my hand and pulled me up.

I hesitantly followed her as she led me into the bathroom. When we got to the full-length mirror, she kept my back to it as she met my gaze.

"Close your eyes," she said.

I rolled my eyes. "Are you serious? Do I have to?"

She nodded. "Yes."

I sighed and obeyed. She took her sweet time counting down from 10, and then she turned my shoulders and pronounced that it was time for me to look. For some reason, I kept my eyes shut as I counted down in my own mind and then opened my eyes. I couldn't believe the person I saw staring back at me.

Sure, Crista wore bold makeup and had spunky clothes, but she had done none of that with me. Instead, my eyes popped in a subtle way. My hair was curled in soft ringlets framing my face. She had picked out a button-up dress with a chunky belt. It wasn't too girly, which I appreciated.

She squealed as she hugged my shoulders. "Cade's going to freak," she said. She glanced up towards the ceiling and said, "I am a genius."

"Yeah, yeah," I said, shooting her an exasperated look. "An artist is only as good as their canvas."

She smiled. "That's true. But it takes a true artist to get their canvas to shine." And then she glanced at her watch. "Oh, I got to go. I promised my mom I would watch my sister tonight so she and Jim could go on a date."

I nodded as I made my way over to my dresser and grabbed a pair of leggings. There was no way I was going to ride Cade's motorcycle in a dress. Crista was busy gathering her things, and a few minutes later she left.

After I slipped on my strappy sandals, I walked downstairs and found my phone. I half expected a text from Cade saying that he had to cancel. I wouldn't blame him if he suddenly got cold feet. Things had been so weird the last couple of days, and I was pretty sure that some distance would cure him of the feelings I was starting to suspect he had for me.

I mean, come on, let's be honest. He and I were about as opposite as two people could be. And was I so delusional that I thought a few stolen moments together could replace a history like ours? From the way my heart raced when I found no text from him, yes, I might be just that delusional.

I found our text chain and decided to take matters into my own hands.

Me: We still on for tonight?

I waited, holding my breath. I allowed myself to linger with the phone on as I waited for him to respond. It didn't take long before my phone pinged.

Cade: Leaving my house right now. Be there in 10

I spent every one of those ten minutes trying to figure out how I was going to handle this evening. Thankfully it was enough time to process my game plan. Even though I was excited to spend time with him, I couldn't lose sight of the fact that he had been my enemy for so long. That he had hurt me for all those years.

As much as I wanted to believe that he'd changed, I had to protect myself. Especially now that my family seemed to be hanging on by a fraying thread. I couldn't handle another relationship breaking down on me. And even though, deep in the corner of my mind, I allowed myself to wonder if Cade and I could ever be more than just enemies or blossoming friends, I couldn't allow those thoughts to surface.

What if I put myself out there just to have him break my heart? I was helping him because it was court ordered. I should distance myself from someone like that.

As I sat in the bay window, waiting for Cade, a noise in the kitchen drew my attention. It was my parents. They must've come home from wherever they'd been. Proof that, yet again, my dad had lied to me. What business trip lasts only one day?

"I know, Ted. But we need to say something. Perhaps

honesty is something that is lacking in our family. We need to say something to the girls. They deserve that." My mom's voice was low and filled with emotion.

I scooted farther behind the curtains and peeked out, hoping no one saw me. Shadows played against the kitchen wall as my parents moved around.

"Julie, it will be fine. They are big girls. But you're right, we should tell them."

Just then, I heard a car door slam. I jumped, whipping around to see Cade heading up our walkway. I didn't want my parents to know that I was skulking in the shadows, eavesdropping. So I slipped out from behind the curtains and turned the front-door handle as quietly as I could.

I stepped onto the stoop—running right into Cade. How had he gotten to the door so fast?

I squeaked and turned, pinching my lips shut. Thankfully, I still seemed to have control of my arms and softly shut the door behind me.

Cade's arms wrapped around my waist as he steadied me. "Geez, Chocolate Milk. With this kind of behavior, one would think that you didn't want to be seen with me."

I shook my head and straightened, trying to ignore how good it felt to have him so close. He smelled good and he looked good. It was a deadly combination.

I stepped back, breaking the connection between us. I brought my finger to my lips and motioned toward his car. Huh, I wondered where his motorcycle was. He walked behind me, and we both got into his car.

He started the engine and pulled out of the driveway. About a minute down the road, he glanced over at me. "Wanna tell me what that was about?"

I kept my gaze trained on my hands and shook my head. "Not really." I could see him stare at me from the corner of my eye. Heat rushed to my cheeks. What was I supposed to do? If I looked at him, he'd know something was wrong. And I wasn't sure I was ready for anyone but Crista to know about my parents.

He sighed and turned his attention back to the road. Then he cursed under his breath. "I forgot my backpack."

That was when I realized I'd forgotten mine too. Shoot. Well, there was no going back. I wasn't ready for whatever truth-telling conversation my parents wanted to have. Right now, I wanted to stay as far away from them as possible.

"It's okay. I forgot mine as well." I glanced over at him and smiled. "I guess we can just go to your portion of the night."

He tapped his fingers on the steering wheel. "Well, we'd be early, and I hate being early. Are you hungry?"

I furrowed my brow. I couldn't help but feel like this was slowly morphing into a date. And I wasn't sure how I felt about that. "Like dinner?"

There was silence in the car before Cade shook his head. "Not a dinner date, if that's what you're asking. I was thinking more along the lines of you're a human and I'm a human. And, as humans, we need to eat."

I studied him. It almost seemed like he was blushing.

But that would be weird and highly improbable. So I pushed the thought from my mind. "Well, if it's strictly because we are the same species and both need to eat, then I guess it would be okay."

His shoulders relaxed as he focused on the road ahead. "Yeah. It's our need to survive."

"Okay." I giggled. As much as Cade bugged me with his constant joking, when I stepped back and just listened to what he said, I realized that he was funny. "Why do you always joke?" I blurted out.

A smile tipped his lips. "I joke?"

I nodded as I looked out the window. "Yeah. It makes it hard to know when you're being serious or not." My voice dropped to a whisper. "Hard to get close to someone like that." My body flushed as I spoke those words out loud.

You could have heard a pin drop in the silence that followed. I nervously pulled on my seatbelt. I needed to work off this anxious energy that was building up inside of me.

I couldn't wait for Cade to say something. "Where's your bike?" I asked. Good. Stick with something simple.

"Um...it looked like it was going to rain, so I thought I'd save you from getting wet. My grandma let me borrow her car." He glanced over, and I could literally feel his gaze sweep over me.

What was he thinking? I wondered if I looked nice enough. I tugged at the hem of my dress. "I hope this is okay. Crista helped me get ready." I closed my eyes. Why did I say that? Now he was going to think that I couldn't dress myself.

"You look nice," he said, his voice was husky.

I swallowed. Oh crap. What was happening?

"I mean, I didn't get a good look when you were ninja-ing out of your house earlier, but..." When he didn't finish his sentence, I glanced over at him. He had that cocky half smile again. "You clean up good, CM."

I pursed my lips. When was I ever going to outgrow that nickname? As if he sensed my frustration, he winked at me. "You take life too seriously, *Penelope*." He exaggerated my name.

I folded my arms. Seriously? How can I go from a pounding heart to complete frustration like this? It was like getting emotional whiplash every other minute. It was exhausting.

"I take life with the right amount of seriousness," I said, rolling my eyes at him.

He tapped the steering wheel as he pulled to a stop at a red light. "When was the last time you did something crazy?"

I wrinkled my nose as I tried to think back. The only thing I came up with was climbing the water tower with him, and I doubted that would prove my point.

So I sighed. "Fine. I'm predictable. I don't like to make mistakes. And I like to follow the rules." The dam inside of me broke, and I continued, the words spilling from my lips. "And what is so wrong about that? Look at you. You're being forced to spend time with me because not taking life seriously got you in trouble."

His lips parted as he watched me. A horn honked from behind us, and he snapped his attention back to the road.

Now that he was no longer staring, my senses came back to me. What the heck had I just done?

CHAPTER TEN

We drove in silence. I studied my hands, wishing that I could somehow go back in time and change what I had said. I could be such a dork sometimes.

I raised my head and parted my lips to say something, but words didn't want to form in my mind. I doubted that "Um...dah..." would translate to "I'm sorry" so I just snapped my lips shut.

When I glanced over at him, I saw that his jaw was set and he was studying the road ahead of him. Man, I must have really ticked him off.

"I want to take you somewhere," he said. His voice was low, and for a moment it sounded as if there was some hurt lurking in the back of his tone.

I settled back in my seat and nodded. "Okay," I whispered. That was the only thing I was going to allow myself to say. I was scared that ugly Penny would rear her head and hurt Cade again. And for some reason, that was the last thing I wanted to do.

It felt so strange.

Five minutes later, Cade pulled into Mick's Diner. It was a train car–turned restaurant. From the large front windows, I could see people either sitting in the booths or at the counter along the far wall. It wasn't the fanciest place, but it served food. And I'd be lying if I said I wasn't starving.

After he turned the engine off, I pushed open my door and stepped out onto the cracked pavement. The sound of his door slamming drew my attention over. He had a strained expression as he glanced toward the diner. Then he dropped his gaze.

What was happening?

"Are you sure this is okay?" I asked as I walked toward the front of the car.

He flicked his gaze over to me and nodded. "Yeah. Why do you ask?"

Before I could stop myself, I said, "You've gone all brooding on me." Heat raced through me as the words floated through the air between us.

His eyebrows rose as he studied me. "Brooding?" He chuckled, which I took as a good sign. He wasn't angry. There was just something going on with him. I guess Cade always seemed like he had everything figured out, so it was strange to think that, maybe, he didn't.

"You get on my case for joking too much, and now

you're not happy because I'm *not* joking?" He stepped closer to me, and we walked to the front doors together.

I tried to ignore how good it felt to have him next to me. Or the fact that he was opening up to me. Why was my heart reacting this way?

Once we got to the front of the diner, he pulled open the door and waved his hand for me to go first. I stepped inside and he followed after me. He guided me over to one of the empty booths and sat. Not sure what to do, I slipped into the seat across from him.

"Are we supposed to just seat ourselves?" I asked, leaning closer to him.

He shrugged and grabbed one of the menus that were tucked between the salt and pepper shakers on the far end of the table. "I doubt they'll kick us out for doing it."

I scoffed. Was that Cade's life motto? *I'll do it until I get kicked out?*

I saw him looking at me from over his menu. I tucked my hair behind my ear and grabbed one for myself. It felt so raw and exposing, him looking over at me like he did. What could he possibly be thinking? Did I want to know?

"Hey, sweetie," a soft voice said to us.

When I turned, I saw the blonde woman from Cade's house smiling down at us. She had her light-blonde hair pulled up into a ponytail. Wisps of hair fell around her face. She wore an apron over her light jeans and t-shirt.

Cade smiled over at her. "Hey, Mom."

She pulled out a notebook and pen. Suddenly, I felt

both of their gazes fall on me. I smiled. "I'm Penelope," I said, reaching out to shake her hand.

Why did I do that? I wasn't really sure, but I might as well commit.

His mom's gaze dropped to my outstretched hand. She took it. "I'm Georgia. Cade's mom."

I nodded. "Yep. I know."

Her eyes widened, and I suddenly felt desperate to explain.

"I saw you a few nights ago when I came over to find Cade. That's when I met Bryson, Olivia, and Rex." A look of recognition passed over her face, but I kept going. For some reason, I didn't want her to think that there was something weird going on between me and Cade. Perhaps I wanted to convince myself as well. "I'm just Cade's tutor and image adjuster."

Blah. That sounded as weird out loud as it had in my head. But what else was I supposed to say? Life coach?

Georgia glanced over at Cade with her eyebrows raised. Relief flooded my body. Good. Let him try to explain it.

He was smiling—of course. Watching me stumble through my words seemed like a favorite pastime for him. "Yep. Principal Connell suggested we work together. You know, since Judge Jones wanted me to get my life in order." He glanced over at his mom and gave her a wink.

Georgia sighed. It was a sentiment I recognized. So, he wasn't just cocky with me. His mother felt it too. "Well, thanks for taking on my son," she said as she raised her pencil and tapped her notepad. "What did you guys want?"

I hadn't really studied the menu, but I didn't want her to stay and hear me say something stupid again, so I picked the grilled cheese with french fries. Cade ordered a burger with all the fixings. His mom wrote it down and disappeared.

I glanced over at Cade. He was leaning back against the booth with his arms folded. He had a satisfied expression on his face.

"So, am I to assume that this really isn't a date, seeing how I just met your mom?" I asked, hoping to sound confident. For a moment, I detected a hint of pink on his cheeks. Had I made him nervous? Or just upset? Either way, it felt good to finally say something that bothered him the same way he was always bugging me.

He straightened and leaned forward, resting his elbows on the table. "Do you want it to be a date?"

My turn. My entire body flushed with heat at his question. Did I want it to be a date? Somewhere in the back of my mind, the word *maybe* floated around. I coughed and fiddled with the napkin dispenser next to me. "I'm not sure how Tiffanii will feel about that. You and I going out on a date." I paused and moved my gaze up to study him. His reaction would give me a good idea of the situation.

He didn't look bothered that I brought up his not-really-but-maybe girlfriend. He shrugged and shifted on his seat. "Eh, I don't care what she thinks," he said, pushing his way out of the booth and standing. He reached out his hand as if he wanted me to take it.

I stared at it. What was going on? I peered up at him.

He sighed. "I'm not going to bite you, CM. I want to show you something."

I hesitated before I placed my hand in his and allowed him to help me up. I tried hard to ignore the tingles that raced up my arm from his touch. I held my breath as he kept my hand firmly in his own. Were we seriously holding hands right now?

"Wh-where are we going?" My voice came out low and breathy. Great. Way to paint a neon sign over your head that says, Your Touch Does Something to Me. I'd never live it down if he suspected that I had feelings for him.

He laughed and turned to wink at me. "Have a little faith."

He led me to the front of the diner and then outside. I stared at our table where his mom had returned to drop off our waters. She didn't look alarmed that we weren't there, so this must be a normal thing.

Once outside, Cade dropped my hand. I fought the groan that grew in the back of my throat. I needed to be okay with the fact that we were no longer touching. I relaxed my expression.

"I'm starving, you know," I said. "You don't want to see what happens to me when I'm hungry."

He glanced back at me. "I think I'll take my chances."

I followed after him as we rounded the building. A

bubbling sound filled the silence. Through the darkness, I could see a statue of a woman. Water trickled down her toga-clothed body and into a pool below. A few multicolored lights shone up through the water, accentuating the places where the drops fell. From where I stood, I could see all the coins that had been tossed in.

I glanced over at Cade, who was studying the water. "What is this?" I asked.

He smiled. "This is the most famous wishing well in the South," he said, jingling the coins he held in his hand.

"Wishing well?"

He peered over at me. "You don't believe in magic?" He laughed as he sat down on one of the benches that surrounded the pool. "I've been coming here since I was a kid. Every time, I throw a coin in."

Not wanting to stand there alone, I made my way over and sat next to him. It was supposed to be innocent, until I realized how close we were to each other. I scooted over to the edge.

"Have they come true?" I asked, keeping my gaze trained forward. I worried what might happen if I looked into his eyes. My resolve to keep my feelings secret just might dissolve on the spot.

"Maybe," he chuckled, his voice low. I turned to look at him. He was studying me as if there were a million words that he wanted to say but wasn't sure how to say them.

And I wasn't sure I wanted him to.

"Can I?" I asked, reaching out my hand. He let a coin

fall onto my palm. I needed to do something to break this spell he had over me.

I stood and made my way over to the pool. I studied the ripples that floated across the surface. A wish. What did I wish for?

The first thing that came to mind was Cade. I knew I wished something about him, I just wasn't sure I was ready to put that out into the cosmos yet. So I went with my parents. Was it wrong that I wished that they would stay together? That this talk about splitting up was just a nasty nightmare?

I didn't want my family to break apart. Sure, we weren't perfect, but that didn't mean I wanted things to change. I hated change. And I hated how helpless I felt. I was used to pleasing people to get what I wanted. And I was beginning to realize that no amount of good grades or teacher recommendations were going to save me from this disaster.

I wish my parents won't break up. I hesitated before I threw the quarter into the water. It plinked as it broke the surface and sunk to the bottom.

"What did you wish for?"

Cade's voice startled me. I glanced over to see that he'd moved from the bench and was now standing next to me. I pushed him with my shoulder.

"You can't tell someone your wish. It's like a law." I glanced over at him.

He raised his eyebrows. "Wow. I didn't know you believed in wishes that much." He winked at me and then turned his attention to the water. A few seconds passed before he held up a coin and flicked it. It flew up above the water and dropped in with a *thunk*.

We stood there in silence. The sound of the water surrounded us. I fought the urge to ask him what his wish had been. I was pretty sure it had something to do with Tiffanii or his family. Though I kind of wanted his wish to involve me.

I wrapped my hands around my arms as I pushed that thought out. There was no need to put that idea in my mind. When I thought too much about Cade, stupid things came out of my mouth.

"Wanna know my wish?" he asked.

Shivers rushed across my skin. I shook my head, worried that, if I spoke, the wrong thing would come out. That I would end up saying, "Yes, but only if it's about me."

"The law," I managed.

He chuckled and leaned closer to me. "That's only if you believe in them. See, I make a wish knowing that if I want it to come true enough, it will."

It almost seemed that with each word, he was leaning closer and closer to me. My heart pounded so hard I could hear it in my ears.

Calm down, Penny. Calm down.

"Well, I believe, so my belief will override yours and the wish won't come true." I kept my gaze forward. At this point, it was really a self-preservation tactic.

"That's too bad, then," he said. The depth of his voice sent shivers down my spine.

I needed to get away. I couldn't feel these things about Cade. "Is our food ready?" I asked, turning to stare at the restaurant.

He pulled back and turned as well. "Probably." Then he glanced over at me. "Ready for some food?"

I nodded and started across the lawn. I didn't stop until I was inside and sitting at our booth. He came in a few seconds later and joined me.

Our food had been delivered, and I was grateful. Eating meant I didn't have to talk. And not talking meant not worrying that my relationship with Cade was changing drastically. I wasn't sure I was ready for that.

CHAPTER ELEVEN

We ate in silence until all of our food was gone. I was grateful that Cade wasn't in a hurry to bring up what had happened by the well. I wasn't ready to face my feelings or his.

I inwardly groaned. Why did I keep using the word *feelings* every time I thought of Cade? It was totally ridiculous and would most certainly never happen. Me and Cade.

Panic rose up in my chest. I needed to get away.

I wiped my mouth with my napkin and set it on top of my plate. Cade was just finishing as well. His plate was empty, and he was drinking the last of his water.

His mom returned and grabbed our plates. "Did you guys want dessert?" she asked, glancing from Cade to me.

"No—" I said.

"Sure." Cade said at the same time.

His mom's eyes widened as she smiled. "I'll come back."

Cade nodded, and his mom headed back into the kitchen with our plates.

"You don't want cake?" Cade asked. He leaned forward on his arms and was studying me.

I shook my head. "I'm not really a cake person," I lied. I loved cake, but I didn't want to stick around even though just hearing the word made my salivary glands kick into overdrive.

He eyed me. "You okay?" he asked.

I pinched my lips together and nodded. "Yep."

"Because it almost seems like you are trying to get away from me."

I feigned shock. "That's not it. I just figured you have a lot going on. Maybe it would be best if we just called it a night." My chest squeezed as the last words left my lips. I didn't want to go home and be alone in my giant, empty house. But being here with Cade was confusing and worrying me.

He met my gaze. "Did I do something wrong?"

Oh man. Why did he have to look so sincere? It was getting harder and harder to hate him. Why did things have to change? I'd been so comfortable in my previous life. And now everything was falling apart.

I fought the tears that threatened to spill. I was rapidly losing control of everything. "Be right back," I called over my shoulder as I stood and hightailed it to the bathroom.

Once I had the door locked, I let out my breath. I could do this. I could continue to hate Cade and keep my parents together. It would just take some work, but I was up to the task.

I turned and faced the mirror. After splashing my skin a few times with the ice-cold water, I felt less and less like I was going to break down at any moment.

I patted my skin dry and took a few deep breaths. The last thing I needed was for Cade to see me cry. He'd know that there was absolutely something wrong with me, and then he'd never leave it alone.

I straightened my hair and blotted under my eyes. After a short countdown, I pulled open the bathroom door to see Cade standing on the other side. His eyebrows were drawn together, and he had a worried look in his eyes. In his hand, he held a small white box in the shape of a piece of cake.

"You okay?" he asked. He raised his gaze to meet mine.

My breath caught in my throat. He was worried.

"I'm okay," I said, giving him a smile and passing by him. When I walked back to the table, I looked for my purse, but I couldn't find it.

"Here," Cade said, reaching out and handing it to me.

"Thanks."

He nodded.

I pulled open the zipper and pulled out a twenty. "How much do I owe?" I asked, glancing around for the check.

When Cade didn't respond right away, I glanced over at him. His jaw was set, and there was a hurt expression on his face. "Don't worry about it. I paid."

No. I couldn't have that. There was no way I wanted to

owe Cade. "It's okay. I should pay for myself." I started walking toward the register.

His hand surrounded my arm, stopping me. "I said, I paid."

I turned, hoping to meet his gaze full force. "Cade, I can pay for myself."

He studied me. "And I can pay for you." He folded his arms.

"I—" This was the most ridiculous fight I'd ever been a part of. So, I found a five in my purse and set it on the table. "Fine. I'll tip."

He started to protest, but I wasn't going to listen to it. "It's just the tip," I said as I challenged his gaze. I gave him a look that said, go ahead, try and stop me.

It must have worked because he clenched his jaw shut and turned, making his way out of the diner. I felt triumphant as I patted the five and turned.

Georgia was standing behind me, studying me. Crap. Had she seen our fight?

"Thanks. The food was great."

She just kept her gaze steady as she nodded. "No problem." Then she narrowed her eyes. "Hey, did you go to junior high with Cade?"

I stared at her. That felt strange. It had been so long ago that I was surprised she even remembered me. "Yeah. I did." Did she know that her son had tortured me for three years? I decided against bringing it up. It felt weird to tattle on her son.

She narrowed her eyes. "Just be nice to Cade. He's been through a lot." She shifted the rag she was holding from one hand to the other. Then she moved past me over to an empty table and began wiping it down.

That was weird. Why was she worried about how *I* would treat *Cade*. Wasn't she supposed to lecture her son? He'd been the one who made fun of me.

I sighed as I turned and made my way out the front door. Once I got outside, I looked around. Where was Cade?

My gaze landed on him. He was leaning against his car with his head tipped back. I blew out my breath as I walked up to him. "Hey," I said.

He glanced at me, and I paused. He looked upset.

I furrowed my brow. "What's wrong?"

He straightened and walked toward me until he was inches from me. He met me with the full force of his gaze. "What was that about?"

I swallowed, completely overwhelmed by his proximity. What was I supposed to say to him when his mere presence knocked me senseless? "What?" I managed.

"You won't ever let me do anything. You always have to say something." He scrubbed his face as he turned away from me. "You drive me crazy."

Oh, no. I wasn't going to let him say something like that and then turn away from me. He was definitely not going to have the last word. "Hang on," I said, following after him. "I drive you crazy? What about you and the whole Chocolate Milk nonsense?" I stepped in front of him so he had to stop.

I folded my arms and tapped my fingers. It both excited me and scared me to confront him like this. But, if he was going to start something, he'd better finish it.

His eyebrows rose as if he was shocked that I would say something about that. He scoffed and glanced away. "You can't ever take a joke, can you?"

I stared at him. A joke? "You had the entire school call me that name. It was humiliating. Talk about taking one dumb accident and forever immortalizing it." I studied him.

He leaned closer to me, and then his expression softened. "You're right. That was wrong of me. But I thought we'd moved on. I figured you knew that I hadn't meant any harm." He stepped around me and leaned against the trunk of his car.

"If you didn't do it to hurt me, then why did you do it?" I was so angry and frustrated that my skin felt hot. What was his deal? Why couldn't I ever figure him out?

He scoffed and turned back to me. "Really, Pen? Really? You can't be that naive."

I swallowed. What was there to be naive about? "Maybe I am," I whispered.

He turned and stepped up to me until we were inches apart. Suddenly, his hand was around my waist and he was pulling me close. My heart pounded as I glanced up at him.

"Wh-what are you doing?" I asked, my voice coming out breathy.

"When we talk, we only end up fighting. I figured I'd

take a different tactic." He leaned closer until his lips were millimeters from mine.

All I wanted to do was kiss him. I rose up on my tiptoes and pressed my lips against his. At first, he held back, surprised that I'd actually kissed him back. But then, the shock must have worn off because he wrapped his arms around me and pressed me so close that it took my breath away.

He deepened the kiss. He wanted to tell me something through this kiss, and I wanted to know what it was. I wrapped my arms around his neck. I needed to hold onto him; I was worried that he would pull back. What if this had been a joke? I wasn't sure I'd survive that kind of humiliation.

A guttural sound came from his throat as he bent down and pulled me up, setting me on the trunk of the car. I wrapped my legs around him and held him close. Why did this have to feel so perfect? Like all we were made to do was argue and kiss.

He began to pull away, but I wouldn't let him. I didn't want to hear whatever he wanted to say. He chuckled as he pulled gently on my arms.

"You gotta let me breathe, Pen," he said.

I relaxed my grip, and he backed up a few inches. I kept my gaze down, too scared of what his expression looked like. If he winked at me, so help me, I was going to punch him.

Suddenly, his hand was there, and his fingers pressed

against my chin. "What's wrong?" He asked. His voice was deep. Caring. It made my heart hurt.

"I'm worried," I confessed. Probably one of the most truthful things I'd ever said to him.

He dipped down and came into my view. It hurt to see the concern in his gaze. This hadn't been a joke to him. What was I supposed to say to that? He was confusing me and surprising me, and it was unsettling.

"Why are you worried?"

I held my breath for a moment before I told him exactly how I felt. Was I being a fool, trusting him with my feelings? "I'm scared you'll hurt me."

His expression turned pained as he met my gaze. "Penny, I would never hurt you."

I wanted to believe him. I wanted to trust him whole-heartedly. But there was something holding me back. "But how can I know for sure?"

He rested his hands on either side of my face and pressed his lips gently against mine. I could feel everything he wanted to say to me. Everything he wanted me to believe. When he pulled back, he kissed my nose, my cheeks, and my forehead.

"Because I couldn't. It's not physically possible for me." He met my gaze, and I saw the force of his intentions. "Now, teasing you, that I can't help. But I will never hurt you."

I pushed him back and he obliged. I focused on him, trying to read his body language. And, even though the sensible portion of my brain told me not to, I trusted him.

And then, the only thing I could think about was how much I wanted to kiss him. I pulled him toward me and crushed my lips against his. He chuckled and allowed me to take charge. It wasn't until he wrapped his arms around my waist and pulled me next to him, that he took over.

CHAPTER TWELVE

You know how everyone says that makeup kisses are the best? Well, imagine you have years of arguments to make up for. We spent a good twenty minutes making out next to Cade's car. It was like we had all this pent-up frustration, and it was finally getting vented out.

When we finally came up for air, he turned and hopped up onto the trunk, where he wrapped his hand around mine and entwined our fingers together. We were both breathing pretty hard.

"Well, Pen, I have to admit, that was..."

I pressed my fingers against my lips and giggled. "Intense?"

He glanced over at me. "Yeah."

I studied our hands, running my finger across his knuckles. "So where do we go from here?" And then I winced.

Since when did I become the *so where do you see this relationship going* type of girl?

Whoa. I couldn't believe that I just put the word *relationship* in a sentence about Cade. But it didn't bother me as much as I thought it would.

When I turned to look at him, he was studying me. "Where do you see it going?" he asked.

I cleared my throat. There was no way I was going to talk about what I wanted before he did. I wasn't ready to be that vulnerable.

"You go first," I said.

He laughed and leaned forward, cradling my hand in his. "Well, I like you. There. Was that what you were waiting for?"

I eyed him. "You like your grandma. Is it that kind of relationship?"

He wrinkled his nose. "Um, no. Gross." His voice trailed off as he reached up and tucked a curl behind my ear. "I like you, like you."

The temperature of my body rose. Whoa. "So, what does that mean? Do you...?" I didn't want to ask him if that meant we were together in the boyfriend-girlfriend kind of way. It felt stupid and dumb. Why couldn't he just tell me what we were?

He pressed his hand against his chest. "Oh, you want me to take charge now? But back in the diner, I was, like, forbidden to buy you food."

I dropped his hand and shoved his shoulder. "I want you

to take charge on the important things. Come on, that's what every girl wants."

He furrowed his brow. "Why are girls so complicated? Men are not mind readers."

I rolled my eyes. There was no way I wanted to have a men-are-from-Mars–women-are-from-Venus talk. Sure, both sexes were complicated, but we didn't need to solve those differences tonight.

So I took a deep breath and allowed myself to be vulnerable. Just as I parted my lips to speak, Cade pressed his finger to them.

"I want us to be together." He focused his gaze as he studied me.

My heart stuttered to a stop as I studied him. Never in my life did I imagine that those few words would mean as much as they did. Especially not when they came from Cade Kelley, my once-sworn enemy.

I didn't trust my voice, so I nodded and leaned forward. He let his hand fall to my lap, and I pressed my lips to his and kissed him gently. I wanted him to know how I felt about what he said.

When I pulled back, his gaze was hazy as he studied me. "Wow," he whispered. "Should I take that as a yes?"

I chewed my bottom lip and nodded.

After a few more kisses, he pulled away. He leaned back with his arm propped up behind him. "What do you want to do now? I mean, I could spend the whole night kissing you, but I don't want to overstay my welcome."

I laughed, leaning forward to wrap my arms around my knees. It wasn't too comfortable, sitting on the trunk, making out. "Yeah, we should probably try to be functioning members of society. We need to learn how to be around other people now that we are...what we are." The last words lingered on my tongue. It was sweet and oddly satisfying to say.

He quirked an eyebrow as if he, too, enjoyed the way that sounded. "Okay. We still have that party to go to, and you look fabulous." He leaned back and bit his lip in an exaggerated way.

I rolled my eyes and shoved his shoulder.

He feigned pain as he grabbed my hand. "Geez, remind me to never compliment you again."

I sighed. There he was. The Cade I knew and, most recently, liked. "I'm game for the party," I said, wiggling my fingers from his grasp.

At first, he fought it, but then, just before he let me go, he used it to pull me closer and press his lips against mine. I leaned back and met his gaze.

He shrugged. "Can't blame a guy for taking advantage of the situation."

I rolled my eyes and jumped off the trunk. "Let's go before you find other advantages to take."

He chuckled as he jumped off and followed me around to the passenger's side. "Oh, honey, we're just getting started." He pulled open the door with a flourishing bow.

Oh man, what had I gotten myself into.

THE BASS COMING from the party could be heard a block away. Cade pulled up along the curb behind a long line of cars. I glanced out and took in the crowded street.

"How long do you think this will last?" I asked.

Cade shrugged. "Eh, probably an hour more before the neighbors go crazy and call the cops." He wiggled his eyebrows. "But we'll have our *fun* until then."

I rolled my eyes at the way he emphasized fun and got out of the car. When he stepped up next to me, his hand engulfed mine and sent shivers up my arm. Was I ever going to get used to his touch? Secretly, I hoped not.

I let him lead me up the sidewalk and across the lawn. After all, this was his friend's party, not mine. Nerves raced through my stomach at that thought. What was his posse going to say when they saw us together? I was the exact opposite of the tattooed, underage smoker group he'd started hanging out with.

I was pretty sure they wouldn't be celebrating that we were finally together.

We stepped into the foyer through the already-open front door. Someone yelled Cade's name from another room, and he nodded toward them in acknowledgment.

There was a loud squeal—which I could only assume came from Tiffanii—and the crowds parted. She sauntered over to us but then stopped when her gaze landed on our hands.

"What happened?" she spat. I was pretty sure that, at that moment, her spit was mixed with venom.

"Tiff, you remember Penny. She's my...good friend," he said, holding up our still entwined hands.

From the death stare she gave me, panic rose in my chest. I tried to wiggle my fingers free, but Cade wouldn't let me go. Desperate for protection, I scooted closer to him. If the crap hit the fan, I was using him as a human shield.

"I remember loser Penny. I don't remember the *good friend* part." Her overly lined lids narrowed as she swept her gaze from Cade back to me.

My breath hitched in my throat. Why had I agreed to come here? I should have known that this was a bad idea. I snuck a look over at Cade. His jaw was clenched, but the rest of his expression remained steady. I tried to channel his confidence as I turned and stared Tiffanii down. Her eyebrows rose as she studied me.

It didn't seem like my intended show of strength was doing its job. She didn't look threatened, and, eventually, her confusion morphed into a mocking smile.

"Well, it's good to see that Penny has some sass." She stepped forward and linked arms with me. "Come on, let me get you a drink," she said, tugging me away from Cade.

Cade tightened his grip, but I nodded that it was okay. I really didn't want to be the rope in their game of tug-of-war. Honestly, I felt that it was better to be on the right side of the devil than in her path. If she wanted to hang on my arm and parade me around the room, so be it.

I was sure I'd survive. Probably.

I could see the reluctance in Cade's expression as he dropped my hand. I shot him a confident smile as Tiffanii pulled me through the crowd. Once he was out of sight, I took a deep breath. I was okay. I could do this.

I peeked over at Tiffanii who was staring straight ahead. I wanted to ask her what her intentions were—'cause apparently, that's what I do with everyone. But I secretly wanted to know if this was, like, another version of the whole, girls all go to the bathroom together thing or if she was taking me to the kitchen to have a knife fight.

I parted my lips, but before I could ask anything, she stepped up to the counter and nodded toward the punch bowl, which sat next to a huge cake. Apparently, this party was for some guy named Peter, and someone was wishing him a "Rocking Birthday."

"Thirsty?" she asked, nodding toward the bright-red punch.

I glanced down, wondering what concoction of alcohol was mixed with it and then shook my head. "I'm good," I said, meeting her gaze.

She furrowed her brow. "What?"

The bass of the music thumped so loud I could feel it reverberating in my chest. I leaned closer and shook my head. "I'm good," I yelled.

"A cup?" she asked, reaching over and grabbing one of the red cups stacked next to the bowl.

"No. I said..." But it was too late. She was already filling up my cup with some of the bright red liquid. Well, no point in trying to tell her I didn't want it. Either she didn't hear me and wanted to be nice—yeah right—or she heard me and just wanted to get me drunk.

When she stuffed the cup into my hand, I smiled over at her. I raised the brim to my lips and pretended to drink. The bitter smell of alcohol met my nostrils, and I tried not to wrinkle my nose.

If I wanted Cade and I to have a fighting chance, I needed to play along with whatever dance Tiffanii was trying to engage me in. Not only was she one of the scariest people in school, she was also psycho. If I didn't want my picture to end up on the news, I needed to make nice with her.

Once she had a cup in hand, she led me to the back door and stepped outside. The music was muffled, which allowed for better conversation. For some reason, I doubted she just wanted to take me out here so we could chat, have a girl-to-girl conversation about boys. I wouldn't be surprised if she took me out here because there were fewer witnesses.

I should have grabbed one of those plastic knives that were sitting next to the cake. Anything was better than nothing.

Tiffanii led me over to a cluster of lawn chairs and took a seat. She brought her legs out and crossed them. Then she lay back and tipped her face toward the sky. Like she was sunbathing, even though it was close to ten o'clock at night.

When I didn't move, she glanced over at me. "Well?" she asked, nodding toward the empty lawn chair next to her.

I studied it and then sat down, keeping my feet planted on the ground for a fast getaway. Whatever she had planned, I'd be ready for it.

A few more minutes of silence ticked by before she sighed and glanced over at me. "So, what's with you and Cade?" she asked.

Bile rose up in my throat. I didn't want to talk to her about Cade. I wasn't even a hundred percent sure what I thought about him or the two of us. Having "girl talk" with Tiffanii felt strange and forced.

"We're…" The words just weren't coming. There was no way I was going to tell Tiffanii that I liked Cade. Like, really liked him. I wouldn't expose my vulnerable side to her. I gathered my wits and settled on, "We're trying things out."

She raised one of her ridiculously thin eyebrows. "Trying things out?" She laughed. It sounded just like the villain in a Disney movie. "Honey. Let me help you with that." She sat up and swung her legs around so they were right in front of me. She rested her elbows on her knees and leaned in. "It's never going to work," she whispered.

I pulled back, trying to distance myself from her. I hated how her one statement made me doubt everything I'd just experienced with Cade. I scoffed and leaned back on one arm. "That's what you think." I pinched my lips together and glanced back over at her.

What was I thinking? Why was I engaging this girl? I

didn't need this insipid girl to like me. I felt like an idiot for even allowing her to bring me out here. I didn't need her permission to like or date Cade. She only had the power I was giving her.

"If that's all you have to say to me, we're done," I said, mustering my courage and standing. I shot a glance down at her, hoping it came across as strong and confident.

She laughed. Loud and mocking. Her eyes turned stormy as she narrowed them at me. "It won't last long. Cade will come back." She reached out and grabbed my hand. Her fingernails dug into my skin. "Cade is not like you. He's like me."

I twisted my arm, but her grasp on me just tightened. "Let me go," I said.

She held on for a moment before she loosened her grip and I pulled free. I glared at her as I stepped to move around the lawn chair.

"Has he told you what he got busted for?" she called out as I passed in front of her.

For some reason, her words caused me to stop. I kept my gaze on the ground but could see her mocking smile from the corner of my eye.

"Ah, he hasn't told you," she said as she leaned back, resting her hands behind her head. "Interesting."

Not wanting to stand there anymore, feeling more exposed than I'd felt in a long time, I walked away as fast as I could. My stomach hurt. My head hurt.

What was with people today?

The memory of the conversation with Cade's mom raced through my head, which was then followed by Tiffanii's words. Didn't anyone believe that Cade and I could make it? Were we fools to think that once-sworn enemies could actually sustain a relationship?

Once I got inside of the house, I found an empty bathroom and locked the door. After kicking the toilet lid down with my foot, I sat on it, pinching the bridge of my nose and squeezing my eyes shut.

I was going to stay here until all the negativity finally loosened its hold on my chest. The only thing I wanted on my mind was Cade.

CHAPTER THIRTEEN

I wish I could say that, after taking a fifteen-minute time-out, I felt better. But I didn't.

Maybe it was because, with what was going on at home and at school, it felt like my life was out of control. I was trying to find something to grab onto while the ocean of life kept pulling me under.

I was drowning, and there was nothing I could do about it.

I wanted to reach out and hang onto Cade. He was rapidly becoming the only person in my life that made any sense—which was strange to admit. But the fear that we would never work and that he'd only break my heart kept gnawing on my mind.

My phone buzzed, and I saw that Cade had texted me. I rubbed my cheeks before I picked it up and swiped it on.

Cade: Where are you? I'm beginning to think that Tiffanii killed you and buried the body (winky face emoji)

She might as well have. Right now, I felt as if she were somehow nailing the coffin shut on my and Cade's relationship. Which is stupid. She didn't have that kind of power. But it felt like she did. I cursed my thoughts.

Me: Haha, nope. In the bathroom.

Just as I sent that off, I winced.

Wow. Way to be romantic, Penny, I scolded myself. I didn't need Cade knowing I was in the bathroom. Plus, it didn't help that I'd been in here for fifteen-plus minutes. He was going to think I had some major stomach issues.

His response came faster than I liked.

Cade: Wow. Everything okay?

I squeezed my eyes shut, forcing down the embarrassment that had crept up into my chest.

Me: Yep. No emergency. Just needed a break from the crowd.

There was a soft knock on the door before I was able to send the last message.

I took a deep breath and shoved every single one of Tiffanii's words to a locked room in my mind. I couldn't let her weasel her way into my thoughts. Her whole goal was to poison my relationship with Cade. If I allowed her to create a wedge between us, then she won. And there was no way that a Tiffanii—spelled with two *i*'s—was going to win in my life.

Just for good measure, I sent the text and stood, blotting

underneath my eyes with my fingertips, in case it wasn't
Cade at the door. But I was pretty sure it was.

Forcing a smile, I turned the door handle and found
Cade on the other side, holding his phone. He must have
just received my text because his gaze was trained on the
screen.

"A break from the crowd, huh?" he asked, glancing up at
me and shooting me one of his stupidly handsome smiles.

In that moment, all my fears and doubts faded away. It
was just me and him.

Instead of answering his question, I wrapped my arms
around his neck and stepped closer to him. I loved how he
responded by wrapping his arms around my waist and
bringing me close. I reveled in the feeling that being next to
him brought.

He just held me for a few minutes. I was grateful that he
didn't ask me any questions. At this moment, my life was too
confusing. I just needed to feel as if someone in my circle
was there for me. Patricia was nonexistent. My parents were
—whatever they'd become. I was rapidly feeling like I was
the only person in my life who was going to stick around.

That is until Cade slipped his way through the wall I'd
built up around my heart. I wanted him in my life, and I was
scared that he was going to leave. That he'd discover just
how ordinary I was and wander off to greener pastures.

"You okay?" he finally asked.

Thankful for the break from my thoughts, I pulled back
and nodded. "Yeah. I am." I smiled up at him.

His gaze was worried. I tried to force a smile, but that just made him study me harder.

"You lying to me, Chocolate Milk?"

I rolled my eyes as I tried to back away. "No."

But his grip tightened as he stooped down to meet my gaze. "You sure? Did Tiffanii say something to you?"

I bit my lip and shook my head. As much as I tried to fight it, Tiffanii's words entered into my mind.

Has he told you what he got busted for?

Why hadn't he told me what he'd done? Was he embarrassed? Didn't he think I could handle it?

"She told you something, didn't she." He cursed under his breath. "What did she tell you?"

Now I needed to know, if it was bad enough for him to get angry over. Before I could stop myself, I pulled back. "She asked me if I knew what you were doing when you got busted. I didn't say anything. But she could tell that you hadn't told me."

He'd loosened his grip, so I took that as my moment to push away and cross my arms. Cade quirked an eyebrow but didn't move to pull me back.

"I guess that I thought it wasn't important, so..." He shoved his hands into his front pockets and shrugged.

My stomach clenched. Did he not think that I could handle something like that? "And you think I'm too goodie-two-shoes to handle whatever law you decided to break? I'm not some fragile person you have to protect from the truth."

I swallowed. Those words probably weren't meant only

for Cade. My parents also needed to realize that keeping things from me hurt almost as much as just saying the words out loud.

Cade raised his hands. Apparently, my slowly rising tone was tipping him off that I really wasn't okay.

"Do you want to know?" he asked.

I sighed, hoping to release some of the tension that had built up inside of me, and nodded. "Well, if we are going to do whatever this is." I waved my hand between the two of us. "We should know everything."

He quirked an eyebrow, and an incredulous expression passed over his face. I shot him a pointed look.

"Okay, well maybe not everything, but the important things."

He smiled and nodded. "I can handle that." He reached out his hand and let it hang in the air.

That wasn't an answer to my question. Trying to hold my hand wasn't telling me the truth. I brought my gaze up to meet his.

He sighed. "I'm going to tell you. Just not here. Let's ditch this party and go somewhere quiet." He leaned closer to me. "I'd rather spend time with you then around these people anyway." He tipped his face slightly so he could meet my gaze.

My insides melted, just a tiny bit. I sighed and nodded. I liked that idea a lot. So I slipped my hand into his and let him lead me out across the lawn. When we got to his car, he opened my door and waited until I slipped onto the seat.

Once I was situated, he shut the door and jogged around to the driver's side.

Ten minutes later, he was parked outside the water tower. I didn't wait for him—I opened the door and climbed out. This place was beginning to feel like our place. Even though I was pretty sure we were trespassing, I wanted to climb that water tower and stare out over the town while my leg brushed against Cade's.

When we were up there, it was just the two of us. Nothing else mattered. Not my family. Not school. Nothing.

And right now, I needed all of those things to fade away.

When we were up on the platform with our legs dangling over the edge, Cade rested his hands on his thighs as he glanced out at the expanse of the town and darkened sky.

I waited for him to start. It felt wrong to be the first to break the silence between us.

"Last year, my dad was arrested." He peeked over at me as if he were worried how I would react.

"Arrested?"

He nodded. "Apparently, he'd been scamming a lot of people at his work. It was bad. He was sentenced to five years in prison."

I cringed. That had to hurt. I couldn't believe that his dad had gone to prison. "I'm sorry," I said.

Cade shrugged. "It wasn't your fault. He was stupid." He sighed as he fiddled with the hem of his shirt. "A few months ago, we also found out that he has a second family."

My stomach dropped. "Cora?"

Cade nodded. "Cora." He swallowed and his Adam's apple bobbed up and down.

I studied the pained expression that passed over his face. My heart squeezed. I felt bad for him. That had to be hard to wrap your head around.

"I'm sorry," I said, reaching out and wrapping my fingers around his hand.

Cade nodded. "Life was pretty rough, and the last thing I wanted was to be at home." He scoffed. "I'd always thought we had a happy life. I mean, we're not rich by any stretch of the imagination, but we were together. And that was all that mattered." His voice drifted off as he began to trace circles around the top of my hand.

My stomach tightened. All the feelings about my family and my parents bubbled to the surface. It seemed as if Cade and I weren't as different as I'd always thought. Sure, I came from the rich side of town, and he lived in the poor side. In the end, we were all just families trying to make things work. We were both affected by heartbreak in the same way.

Wow. I'd been so dumb. How could I have hated Cade for so long? Man was I naive.

"I'm sorry," I whispered.

Cade shrugged. "I fell in with the Buddha and Tiffanii crowd. I wanted so badly to distract myself—to not feel anything. My mom was a wreck. I didn't want to be home, where I was reminded of how we used to be." He scrubbed his face. "Buddha took me in. Made me feel welcome." His shoulders slumped. "It got to the point where I would do anything, just to please them."

A tingle started at my spine and raced across my body. This was the moment. He was going to tell me what he'd done to get in trouble.

"They came to me with a plan. An initiation so to speak. They asked me if I was family." He closed his eyes as if that word felt strange. "I told them I was. There was nothing I wouldn't do for my family."

My heart was torn. On the one hand, it was admirable that he felt that kind of loyalty. On the other, he'd broken the law. I think I would struggle with that if someone asked me to jeopardize my future.

He sighed. "Buddha has gotten in trouble before. Apparently, there was this judge that he really hated, Judge Jones." He looked over at me. I recognized the name, but didn't know him personally. Cade continued, "He wanted to get back at him. The judge has a 1957 Chevy Bel Air. It's his pride and joy. We were going to steal it. Joy ride around town in it and bring it back—or at least, that was what Buddha said he wanted to do."

Cade leaned back on his arm and glanced over at me. I kept quiet, waiting.

"My job was to break in and get the car out of the judge's garage." He scrubbed his face. "I know some about cars because I've helped my dad restore a few. I wanted to prove myself to Buddha, so I agreed. I broke into the garage and was halfway through hot-wiring it when the judge found me."

I hadn't noticed that my heart had picked up speed. When he finished his last sentence, my stomach squeezed. "Wow," was all I could say.

"Yeah. He was pissed." Cade straightened and rested his arms on the railing in front of him, moving his gaze to study the scenery around us.

I couldn't help but watch him. I felt so bad that he had to go through that. "So what happened?"

"Judge Jones took pity on me. Realized who my mom was. Apparently he and my grandma had a thing a long time ago. He decided not to press charges, but he did give me some stipulations: Bring up my grades. Fall in with the right crowd. Do what I'm supposed to." He glanced over at me. There was a hint of worry behind his gaze. "So, what do you think about me now? Still want to be with me?"

I hesitated as I met his gaze. It was the strangest feeling. Even though he'd told me that he'd broken the law, I didn't care. This was Cade we were talking about. The guy that I'd hated so much for so long just to realize that, perhaps, he was the perfect guy for me. He could tell me that he was an alien from another planet, and I would still like him.

I leaned forward and pressed my lips to his. After a few seconds, he chuckled and pulled back.

"That's a yes?"

I nodded and Cade leaned forward again. This time, he

didn't hold back. His lips moved against mine as he pulled me close. In that moment, no one mattered. Just me and Cade.

As his fingers moved to the back of my neck to cradle my head, I was pretty sure I was never going to be the same. Cade Kelley had changed me. Nothing else mattered but being with him. I'd face my mess of a life tomorrow.

Tonight, I was here.

CHAPTER FOURTEEN

The early morning light shone through my eyelids, and I bolted up. I glanced around and groaned.

I was still up on the water tower. And I was still with Cade.

After our intense emotional talk last night, we lay down next to each other to count the stars and just talk. He told me about his siblings and his new half-sister. I kept information about my family light. I didn't want to overshadow what he'd told me. Plus, I wasn't even sure how I felt about it all, and I was pretty sure he'd press me for information. Was it wrong that I just wanted him to think that I had everything figured out?

As I grew tired, he suggested a Netflix movie on his phone and I agreed. My house was the last place I wanted to be. I snuggled into him, and we must have fallen asleep.

"Hey," I said, shaking his shoulder.

Cade's eyes opened and when his gaze landed on me, he smiled. My stomach instantly turned to Jell-O. Yeah, I'd made the right choice with Cade.

"Morning," he said, sitting up. He ran his hand through his hair and glanced around.

When he peered back at me, I found myself nodding. This was the first time I'd ever slept next to a boy. I wasn't sure how I felt about it. I really wasn't sure how my parents would feel about it.

"What's wrong, Chocolate Milk?" he asked in his flirty and teasing tone.

I swallowed as I mustered a glare. "I just—have never slept with a boy before." Heat raced to my cheeks as the words tumbled from my lips.

Okay, so that wasn't the best choice of words.

He quirked an eyebrow. Of course.

"Wow, Penny. What do you think is going on around here?" He wiggled his eyebrows and gave me an incredulous look.

I rolled my eyes and shoved his shoulder. "I didn't mean it like that. It's just, I didn't expect to fall asleep next to you." I stretched and pain radiated down my back. I guess sleeping on a grate would do that a person.

He wiggled his eyebrows, and he reached into his pocket to pull out a pack of gum. He offered me some and I took it.

"Well, I enjoyed it," he said, wrapping an arm around his knee and studying me.

How was he always so relaxed?

I let out my breath slowly. I liked that we could be so honest and open with each other. My features must have softened because his grin grew wider.

"You enjoyed it too," he said.

I dropped my jaw. "I did not."

He reached up and grabbed my hand. In one swift movement, he pulled me down onto him. I giggled as his arms wrapped around me and brought me close. "Yes, you did," he said, burying his face in my neck and kissing me.

Shivers erupted across my skin. I reveled in the feeling of being next to him. I relaxed and wrapped my arms around him. He held me for a few more minutes before he moved back; I stifled a groan.

I wanted to stay here forever. Being with him brought me more happiness than anything else in my life.

"I should get some food in you and then bring you home. If we are going to make a go of this"—he motioned between the two of us—"then I want your parents to like me. Bringing you home in the wee hours of the morning probably isn't the best way to gain their trust."

At the mention of my parents, my stomach soured. I forced a relaxed look as I shrugged. "Eh, they probably haven't even noticed that I'm gone."

When his brow furrowed, I realized that probably hadn't been the right thing to say. I laughed it off, but he didn't look like he bought it.

"Penny, wha—"

"Breakfast?" I said, interrupting him.

He closed his lips and studied me. I gave him a look that said, *please don't ask me.* That must have come across because he just nodded and helped me up. Once he was standing, he made his way down the ladder of the water tower, and I followed after him.

When my feet landed on the ground, he took my hand and we walked over to his car. He opened my door and I climbed in. Once he was inside, he started the car and took off down the road.

Ten minutes later, we pulled into the parking lot of McDonald's. It wasn't the healthiest breakfast, but I was starving.

"Ready for some food?" he asked.

I nodded as I pulled on my door handle and got out. Once we were inside, I excused myself and headed to the bathroom. I washed my hands as I studied my reflection. Man, I looked terrible.

My makeup was smudged, and my hair was crazy. I took a moment to clean up and run my fingers through my hair. After I looked somewhat presentable, I grabbed my phone from my purse. I had ten texts. Five were from Crista asking me how the night went. Two were from my mom and three from my dad.

My parent's texts went from freaked out to calm. Mom said she talked to Crista and was happy one of us was responsible. Apparently, Crista had covered for me and told her that I slept at her house.

It felt weird to get separate texts from my parents. It was

like a visual manifestation of their separation. Why wouldn't they just ask each other about me?

Emotions rose up in my throat. Because they weren't together anymore. I doubted Dad had even been at the house last night.

Not wanting to face that right now, I threw my phone back into my purse and pulled open the bathroom door. I fought back the tears that brimmed on my lids. I couldn't think about that right now. My parents weren't going to ruin what I had with Cade.

If I allowed myself to dwell on what was happening to my family, Cade would find out. And I was so close to breaking that I couldn't speak the words out loud. Maybe it was because I wasn't ready to face it.

Cade was standing in line when I joined him. We ordered, got our number, and stood off to the side while we waited. Cade wrapped his arm around my waist and pulled me close. I rested my head on his chest. Right here, everything was perfect.

Movement by the door drew my attention. Dad was holding the door for someone. A woman with dark hair and caramel-colored skin.

I blinked. What?

No. That couldn't be Dad. And that most definitely was not Mom.

I straightened, pulling away from Cade.

He protested, but I didn't hear him. My ears were ringing as my vision went hazy. I massaged my temples, hoping to alleviate the headache that was pounding against my skull.

There was no way I was seeing this.

Dad leaned down and kissed the woman on her lips, and I wanted to scream. But my throat was so constricted, no sound could come out.

There they stood. In the doorway of McDonald's. Kissing.

Vomit rose up in my throat. I turned and headed for the side door. I needed some fresh air. I didn't want to throw up on the floor. Dad would most certainly see me, and I'd have to confront him. And that was the *last* thing I wanted to do.

Cade must have been following me because, as soon as I got outside, I felt his hand around my arm. I fought him, pulling away so I could put some distance between me, Dad, and Dad's—whatever she was. Bleh. Even thinking that sentence made my skin crawl.

"Penny," Cade's voice broke through my cloudy mind.

I shook my head, keeping my gaze tipped to the ground. I couldn't face him right now. I knew the moment I looked into his eyes, I'd break down. I'd become a blubbering fool. and I couldn't do that right now. I needed my strength.

But Cade wouldn't let me go. Instead, he pulled me to his chest and crushed me in a hug.

Even though every fiber of my being wanted to run as far away as I could, being held by Cade relaxed me, and I collapsed into him.

I cried.

Hard.

The tears flowed. All the pent-up frustration and pain from the moment I'd realized that Mom and Dad weren't in love anymore to my rollercoaster relationship with Cade, they all came out in the sobs I muffled with his shirt.

I don't know how long we stood behind the McDonald's while drive-through cars passed by us, but it lasted as long as I had tears. Once I was sure I had nothing left, I pulled back.

My stomach dropped when I saw the huge wet spot on his shirt, smeared with mascara. I was pretty sure I looked as terrible as I felt. Hoping to salvage myself, I wiped at my eyes and nose.

When I glanced up to meet Cade's gaze, I saw him studying me. He had a look of concern on his face. When he met my gaze, he smiled in a "you're upset, and I'm really not sure why, but I want to be supportive" kind of way.

I took a deep breath and released it. "I saw my dad," I said. My voice came out in a whisper.

Cade leaned closer.

I cleared my throat and tried again. "I just saw my dad."

He pulled back and studied me. "What? Here?" He peered around me as if he were trying to see into the restaurant. Which was silly because there was no way he'd be able to see from where we stood.

I nodded. "Yes. Here. Back there." I waved toward the exit we'd just left.

He glanced over at me. "But... Why did that make you upset?"

I swallowed, forcing the next words to touch my lips and escape out into the air. "He was with another woman."

I pinched my lips shut. I couldn't believe this was actually my life.

Cade's expression morphed into one of understanding. He scrubbed his face with his hands as he looked up at the sky. "Oh, man. Pen, I'm so sorry." He blew out his breath and returned to studying me.

I shrugged and pulled at the leaves of the bush next to me. I didn't want his pity. I didn't want him to say that everything would be better. I wanted him to tell me that this sucked. That my parents sucked because they were doing this to me.

"How long has it been going on?"

I swallowed. If I were honest with myself, a long time. I could tell my parents were drifting apart, but a part of me had always hoped that maybe I was just crazy. That my parents were still in love and not destined for divorce like so many of my friends' parents.

We had money. We had a good house and a good life. What else did my parents need? If anyone could make things work, it was us.

"A while," I whispered as I plucked a leaf from the bush and crumpled it in my hand. After a few seconds, I let it fall to the ground.

"Did you know?"

I shrugged. "Kind of."

He fell silent, and I glanced over, wondering what he was thinking. He had a contemplative expression.

"Why didn't you tell me?" he finally asked.

I shrugged as I grabbed another leaf. "I don't know. I guess you were sharing your stuff, and I didn't want it to seem like I was overshadowing that."

He reached out his hand and engulfed my elbow. His touch was warm and supportive. I loved and hated it at the same time. He shouldn't be nice to me; I'd lied to him. I'd even thought, on many occasions, that I was better than him.

That was not the case. At all.

I broke contact as I folded my arms. I guess I needed space, but I also wanted to protect myself. Keeping my distance from him seemed like the best idea.

"Do you want me to take you home?"

I nodded, squeezing my arms against my chest. "Yeah. I'm tired." And there was no way that I wanted to stick around here. Not when Dad was basically making out with the new woman in his life.

Just thinking those thoughts made me sick.

As if he sensed that I didn't want to be touched, Cade held his arm out and motioned for me to follow. We walked to his car in silence. He started the engine and pulled out from the parking lot onto the main road. I kept my gaze down as we drove past the McDonald's windows.

I didn't want to see Dad. If I saw him happy without Mom, Patricia, and me, I just might break. And I wasn't sure how I would get put back together again.

CHAPTER FIFTEEN

As soon as Cade dropped me off at home, I slipped inside and went right up to my room. I wasn't hiding because I was worried that my parents would find out I'd spent the night with a boy. I was worried that my suspicions would be verified, and my family would break into pieces right before my eyes.

I slipped out of my clothes and climbed into bed. I was going to stay here for the rest of my life. Here, I was safe. I closed my eyes and allowed the softness of my mattress and the exhaustion I felt overtake my body as I fell asleep.

I didn't wake up until I heard a knock on my door. I lifted my head, wondering if I'd heard right. I stilled, straining to hear. The knock came again.

I groaned as I buried my head under my pillow. There was no way I wanted to talk to whoever was on the other side of the door. "Go away," I muttered, not really caring if they heard me or not.

I heard the door handle turn, and Mom's soft voice filled the silence. "Penny? Can we come in?" she asked. Her voice grew louder, which I took as her entering my room.

"No," I whispered.

"Are you awake?"

I felt a hand on my shoulder. It took all my strength not to pull away and attempt to disappear under my covers like I did when I was little. Sure, I shouldn't be treating Mom like this, but with the bomb I was pretty sure she was about to drop on me, I couldn't help it.

My life was changing, and I wasn't ready for it. At all.

"No," I muttered.

I heard her sigh as the mattress tipped. She'd sat down on my bed. "Penny, your dad and I need to talk to you."

I pinched my eyes shut, wishing I was somewhere else.

"Can you come out from under there?"

"No," I said again, hating that my voice sounded so unsure. Why couldn't I be stronger? Since when had I become this weak?

"Please?"

Guilt rose up in my chest, so I pulled the pillow off my face and sat up. "What?" I asked, cringing at the bite in my tone.

Mom's eyes widened as she pulled back slightly. Why did she look so surprised? Did she actually think that I didn't know what was going on? "Penny, are you okay?"

I swallowed. The emotional lump in my throat constricted.

Hold it together, Penny. Don't let them see just how much this is breaking you.

"Yeah. I'm fine."

She raised an eyebrow. "Where were you last night?"

I stared at her. What was I supposed to tell them? That I'd spent the night with Cade? Nope. I couldn't tell her that. He was the only thing that was keeping me sane, and if she found out I'd been with a boy, I'd be grounded for eternity. So I just shrugged and picked some lint off my comforter. "I was with Crista."

Mom folded her hands and nodded. And that was it. She believed me. Probably because lying wasn't something I normally did. It was amazing how much I'd changed.

"Next time, call will you? I was worried. And your dad"—she glanced over at him. He was leaning with one shoulder on the door frame—"he was pretty worried too."

I tried not to glare as I glanced briefly over at him. Did she know that Dad had a girlfriend? Was this the reason they were no longer together? Because Dad had gone off and started a new life with her.

Ugh. My stomach twisted. I didn't want to have to be the person to inform her of Dad's indiscretions.

"Okay," I said. I wished she would just hurry up and tell me that they were getting a divorce. That we were now a broken family and I was going to have to pick which house to live at. I looked at her expectantly.

Mom furrowed her brow but didn't dwell on it. She rubbed her thighs with her hands as she glanced over at Dad. "Your father and I wanted to discuss something with you."

I swallowed. Here we go.

"We are...well..." She gave me a forced smile. "We're separating...for good."

And there it was. The four little words that meant we were no longer a family. Tears brimmed my eyes as fury rose up inside of me. All this time I'd believed that we were happy. I was such a fool.

I turned my attention to Dad. He had a sorrowful expression as he shot me a sad smile. I glared at him. This was all his fault.

"It's because of you," I said, not suppressing my anger anymore. I wanted him to know that I knew. Even if Mom didn't.

Mom's hand rested on mine. "Oh, no. It's not your dad's fault. It's both of us. We've grown apart. We aren't...happy."

That last statement hurt more than anything. My parents were no longer happy with us being a family. Suddenly, I needed to get out of there. I threw my covers off and grabbed a change of clothes. Mom called after me, but I ignored her. I was done with them. I'd spent so much of my life working to make them happy. To make them proud. And yet, there was nothing I could do to keep them together. They were getting a divorce, and that was final.

I was going to live with Mom while Dad went off and

married his mistress, and he'd start a new family and completely forget about us. I'd seen it so many times. They literally made movies about it.

Once I was in my bathroom, I shut the door. I needed a shower, and then I was leaving. I was going to drive to Cade's house and never come back. What did it matter anyway? This wasn't where I belonged.

Mom and Dad must have gotten the memo that I didn't want to talk anymore because, by the time I got out of my twenty-minute shower, they were gone. I dressed, put on some makeup, and pulled my hair up into a messy bun.

I glanced at the mirror when I was done. It was rushed, but at least I didn't look like I'd spent the night sleeping on the metal grate that surrounded the water tower.

Butterflies flitted around in my stomach at the thought of meeting up with Cade again. I grabbed my keys from my purse as I slipped down the stairs. Once I was in the van, I started the engine up and drove the twenty minutes to Cade's house.

I didn't see his motorcycle in the driveway, but I got out anyway. I crossed the front lawn, and, when I got to the front door, I knocked. A few seconds ticked by before the door was opened by the same little blond boy from earlier. His eyes widened as he looked me over.

"Cade's not here," he said, shoving the sucker he was holding back into his mouth.

I glanced behind him. "Is he at work?" Why was I so dumb? Of course he was there.

He nodded.

I smiled down at him. "What was your name again?"

He pulled the sucker from his mouth. "Bryson."

I stuck out my hand. I might as well introduce myself to his family. I was pretty sure that I wasn't going anywhere. "I'm Penelope, but you can call me Penny."

Bryson studied my hand and then raised his gaze to meet mine. "Cade said to call you Chocolate Milk."

I rolled my eyes. Of course. At least, it'd become more of a term of endearment than an insult. I smiled at Bryson. "You can call me that too."

He shrugged, shoved the sucker back into his mouth, and slapped my hand in an awkward high-five.

"Shorty, who's at the door?" A quiet, female voice asked. I recognized it as Cade's mom.

"Hey," I said, nodding toward her as she rounded the corner.

She stopped and her eyes widened. "Penny," she said as she glanced around and then focused back on me. "What are you doing here?"

Why did I always feel so uncomfortable around her? Like she was judging me or something. Did she know we'd fallen asleep together? "I was looking for Cade."

She walked up to Bryson—who was also called Shorty apparently—and shooed him from the door. Bryson didn't protest and disappeared down the hall she'd just come from.

"Well, he's not here," she said, folding her arms and staring at me.

"Yeah, Bryson said that." I parted my lips, wondering if I should say more. But then I decided against it and just glanced around.

When she didn't respond, I nodded toward my car. "I should go," I said.

His mom glanced toward where I'd motioned and then back to me. "That would be best."

I hesitated. What did that mean? "Thanks," I said, partly out of habit—and partly because I wanted his mom to like me.

I gave her a weak smile before I turned and hurried down the steps. Just as I was halfway across the lawn, her voice caused me to stop. Turning, I saw her step out onto the stoop.

"Penny?" she called again.

"Yeah?"

"Are you free for dinner tonight?"

I hesitated and then nodded. "Yes." There was no way I was going home for dinner. Plus, I needed to win her over. So, I smiled even though she didn't look at all thrilled that she'd just invited me.

"Seven o'clock," she called out before turning and heading back into the house.

I stared at the now empty stoop, wondering what that had been about. Why was she so displeased with me? What had I done?

Before I went crazy trying to figure her out, I climbed into the car and started the engine. I was tired of ridiculous adults who did ridiculous things. Right now, I was excited to see Cade. That was all that mattered.

Whenever I was with him, things felt better. I was better.

It wasn't long before I was pulling into the diner's parking lot. It was the early dinner rush. All the tables were filled with stressed-out parents trying to control hyped-up kids. I parked in the only open spot and got out.

I scanned all the faces, hoping to find Cade. He was standing next to a table, getting french fries thrown at him while he tried to take an order. I giggled as I walked up, thankful he didn't notice me.

I took an empty seat at a far table. The family next to me glanced over but, thankfully, returned back to whatever they were doing. I grabbed out my phone and swiped it on. I'd just wait here until things calmed down. After all, I had nowhere else to go.

Fifteen minutes later, the family left, leaving me alone at the table. I'd found a book on my phone and gotten lost in it. I didn't notice Cade standing next to me until he cleared his throat.

"Hey, when did you get here?" he asked.

I glanced up at him and smiled. "Not that long ago."

He rested both hands on the table as he dropped his head down.

"Tired?" I asked.

He glanced up at me and nodded. "It's been insane

here." Then he leaned closer to me. "And I spent the night with this amazing girl. We didn't get much sleep."

Ha. If I wasn't so emotionally exhausted, I might have told him how dirty that sounded. Instead, I reached out and covered his hand with mine. "I'm sorry it's been busy." I wasn't sure I had the energy to say anything more.

He shrugged and then moved to sit across from me.

"Is it your break?" I asked.

"It is now. They can all wait a minute while I talk to you."

I peered around at the other customers. They seemed too preoccupied with their conversations to notice that Cade had sat down. I was thankful for that. I needed to talk to him. I needed to have him tell me everything was going to be okay.

"Thanks," I said, my emotions bubbling up inside.

He smiled. "Of course." Then he furrowed his brow. "Everything okay?"

I pushed around some abandoned salt on the table. "My parents had the talk with me." I glanced up to see worry cross his expression. Then it morphed into a teasing smile.

"Didn't they cover that in fifth-grade health?"

I rolled my eyes. "Not that kind of talk. The divorce talk." I winced as that word lingered in the air.

He pulled his hand out from under mine and rested it on top. His warmth spread up my arm and exploded throughout my body. I loved how, with one gesture, he could comfort me.

Someone from the crowded tables called his name and we glanced in their direction. A man waved Cade over.

"I should go," he said, smiling over at me. "Wait around a while?"

I nodded. "Sure."

He squeezed my hand before standing and weaving his way through the tables.

Thirty minutes passed before he came back and handed me a chocolate shake. I smiled as he leaned down and brushed a kiss on my cheek. Before I could say anything to him, he disappeared again.

Being here helped me feel complete. I didn't need affirmation from anyone else but Cade. Adults just failed you, and I was tired of trying to earn their approval.

I drummed my fingertips on the table as I drank my shake. This was where I belonged. I was happy. Sort of.

CHAPTER SIXTEEN

The sun had dipped down behind the trees before Cade collapsed on the seat next to me. He rested his head on his arm and groaned. Out of instinct, I reached out and rubbed his back.

I loved that I could touch him now. That I didn't have to worry about anything. I liked Cade and he liked me.

"You okay?" I asked.

He shrugged as he lifted his head to glance over at me. "I am now."

Heat raced to my cheeks at his comment and the unabashed way he stared at me. He leaned forward and kissed my cheek. I loved that he was so sweet.

When he pulled back, he rubbed his temples. "How are you feeling?" he asked.

I shrugged. Truth was, I hadn't thought about my

parents in the two hours I'd been here. I wasn't going to let their toxicity ruin my evening.

"I'm fine. Now that I'm with you." I leaned over and rested my head on his shoulder.

He pulled back, forcing me to sit up. "Pen, really?"

I nodded, hating the frustration that rose up in my chest. "Yeah. I'm fine."

He narrowed his eyes as he studied me. "You can be honest with me."

Heat coursed through my body. Why was he pushing this? "I am."

He hesitated before he nodded. "Okay."

I could tell he didn't believe me, but I chose to let it go. I set an elbow on the table and rested my head on my hand. I drew circles on the tabletop. "So I went to your house to find you."

He glanced over at me. "Really?"

I nodded. "Your mom invited me to dinner. Said we should be there by seven."

He peered down at his watch. "We should go then. I'll tell Jordan that I'm leaving for the night." He stood and made his way over to his leggy blonde coworker. She nodded and he disappeared into the back. A few minutes later, he emerged, sans apron, and walked over to me.

"Ready?" he asked.

I nodded and followed him to his motorcycle. For some reason, all I wanted to do was hang on to him as he flew down the road. My parent's minivan just couldn't compete.

"Will you bring me back to get my car?" I asked as I took the helmet he handed me.

He pretended to mull that over. "Let me see. Give you a ride, which means you sit right behind me, or have you drive your own car." He tapped his chin. "Hmm."

I shoved his shoulder after I buckled the clasp under my chin. "You're so funny," I said.

He grinned and grabbed my hand. He pulled me close. "Of course I want you next to me," he said.

Tingles erupted across my skin as his words washed over me. "Glad to hear it," I said.

Once he was on the motorcycle, I climbed on after him. I didn't wait to wrap my arms around his chest. I could feel his heartbeat, and his warmth washed over me.

He started the engine and peeled out of the parking lot. It didn't take long before he was pulling into his driveway. After he turned the motorcycle off, I swung my leg over and stepped onto the grass. He joined me, taking my helmet.

He set our helmets on the seat and grabbed my hand. He entwined my fingers with his as he led me up the walkway to the front door. He didn't ring the doorbell—of course. He just turned the handle and pushed inside.

The smell of garlic bread and marinara sauce wafted out. I inhaled. It smelled so good.

He kicked off his shoes, and I followed suit. Then he led me around the corner and into a large, lived-in living room. Toys were strewn all over the place.

Cade's little sister—whose name I couldn't remember—

was sitting on a chair, with her knees brought up. She was reading a book and twirling her hair with her finger.

"Hey, Tulip," Cade said.

Tulip—I was pretty sure that wasn't her real name—peeked at him from above her knees. A smile spread across her lips as she closed her book and stood on the cushion.

"Monster!" she squealed as Cade picked her up and squeezed her.

I glanced between the two of them. Tulip? Monster? Shorty? Was this a family of nicknames?

As if Tulip suddenly realized that I was standing next to Cade, her eyes widened. "Hey, you were here earlier," she said as Cade set her down.

She appraised me with her gaze.

"I'm Penny," I said.

Her brow furrowed as she glanced back at Cade.

"Chocolate Milk," he said with a half smile.

Tulip giggled, covering her mouth with her hand. "Right." She reached out. "Olivia, but Cade calls me Tulip."

I shook her hand, glancing over at Cade. I quirked an eyebrow. What was with the nicknames?

"It's a Kelley family tradition. Everyone gets a nick-name." His voice trailed off as he studied me.

Emotions clung to my throat.

A Kelley family tradition.

But Cade gave me mine a long time ago. What did *that* mean? Here I thought he'd been making fun of me. But maybe I was wrong? I was going to have to ask him about it later.

He wrapped his arm around my shoulder and pulled me close, whispering in my ear, "Don't read too much into it, CM."

The warmth of his breath and the closeness of his body sent shivers down my spine.

I tried to shrug like it didn't mean anything, but that was a lie. It meant something. And I liked that it did.

Cade's mom called from the kitchen that dinner was ready. Olivia turned and made her way into the next room. Cade kept his arm wrapped around me as he led me into a small dining room.

Cade's two brothers were sitting on one side of the table. They were goofing around with Transformer action figures. Fake gun and explosion sounds filled the air.

Cade's mom kept shushing them.

An elderly woman sat on the far end. A pair of dark-rimmed readers were perched on her nose. She had a small paperback book sandwiched between her fingers. Her salt-and-pepper hair was pulled back into a bun.

I glanced over at Cade, who'd led me over to an empty chair.

"That's my grandma. She's been here since my dad..." His voice trailed off.

I nodded. He didn't need to tell me; I understood.

He shot me a thankful smile and pulled out my chair so I could sit down. Once I was situated, he sat next to me.

"Now, who is this?" his grandma asked.

I glanced over at her. Her warm brown eyes made me feel instantly welcome.

"This is Penny. She's my..." He quirked an eyebrow at me. We really hadn't discussed the nitty-gritty details of our relationship. I was kind of hoping he'd fill in the blank.

"We're friends," I blurted out. I couldn't stand the silence.

She nodded. "Nice to meet you Penny. I'm Jennifer." She pulled her readers from her nose.

"No you're not," Shorty piped up. "You're J-money."

I snorted. I was not expecting that.

Jennifer gave Shorty an exasperated look. Then she leaned over to me.

"They're convinced I'm rich, so they bequeathed the name, J-money, on me." Her expression looked exasperated, but there was laughter there too. I could tell she loved her grandkids.

"I like it," I said.

Cade's mom appeared from the kitchen carrying a large casserole dish with two oven-mitt covered hands. Steam rose off the top as she set it down in the middle of the table. Tater tots dotted the top.

"I hope you like tater tot hotdish," she said as she slipped her hands from the oven mitts and set them on the buffet behind her.

I nodded. "What person doesn't?" I gave her a smile, but she just raised an eyebrow.

Man, this woman really doesn't like me.

I wish I could say that it didn't bother me, but it did. A lot.

"Don't mind old Joyce over there. She's been crabby since—well, since she was born," J-money said as she leaned over to me.

"Mom," Joyce said, giving her a pointed look.

J-money held up her hands. "I'm just helping the poor girl out." She leaned back, resting against the chair. "I've always said that I feel bad for the girl that Cade brings home. She'll have to battle you for the boy."

"Mom." Joyce's voice was sharper now.

Heat crept across my skin. What was happening?

The feeling of Cade wrapping his hand around my fingers raced up my body. Suddenly, everything was calm. I felt like I could breathe again. I glanced over at him and saw a smile play on his lips.

After the food was dished up, I had to drop Cade's hand to eat. I enjoyed sitting there, listening to his family talk. Olivia went on and on about a school project she was working on. His two younger brothers goofed off as their mom scolded them.

It was hectic, but I enjoyed it. Ten times better than being at my house. Here, I could just sit back. I didn't feel like I had to contribute or worry about what my parents weren't saying in their exasperated looks and weighty sighs.

And Cade was here. I never would have thought that

one sentence would bring such peace to my soul. I needed him. More than I needed anyone ever before.

Which was so strange. So, so strange.

After my plate was cleaned, I sat back and set my fork on top of it. It seemed like everyone else was finished because the volume only increased.

Joyce told the boys that their punishment for goofing off was to clear the table. They fought for a moment over who got to grab my plate. Shorty won and triumphantly brought it into the kitchen.

Cade pushed his chair back and nodded toward me. "Come on," he said.

I glanced up at him and then followed.

From the corner of my eye, I saw Joyce part her lips to protest, but J-money must have shot her a look because she leaned back and closed her mouth.

Hoping that this was okay, I followed after Cade.

As we slipped down the hall, I heard his mom call after us, "Door open, Cade."

He nodded, but kept his gaze trained on me. "Yeah, Mom."

"Joyce, leave the poor boy alone," J-money responded.

I smiled. I liked his grandma.

He brought me up the stairs and pushed open his bedroom door. I stood in the hall, staring in.

The room was immaculate. Never in a million years did I think it would be this pristine.

"You're a neat freak," I said, glancing over at him.

He winked at me and entered, flopping down on his bed. "Should I be insulted that you figured me for a slob?"

I shook my head as I made my way over to the desk chair that sat in the far corner. "No. You're a guy. I just figured all guys were messy." I twisted in the chair. "I mean, your room is cleaner than mine."

He chuckled as he sat up, resting back on his arm. "That worries me, Chocolate Milk."

I shrugged.

The room fell silent. When I glanced over at him, I wondered what he was thinking. Why was he such a mystery to me?

"What?" I asked.

He shrugged. "Just wondering what you're thinking."

I spun around a few times. "I like your house."

"Oh really?"

I stopped to study him. "Yeah. Why is that such a surprise?"

A look passed over his face. There was something that he wasn't telling me.

"Cade?"

He picked at some imaginary lint on his comforter. "I guess, since I've known you, you always acted like my side of town was less than..." He squinted as if he were trying to figure out the right thing to say. "Desirable?"

I winced at his word. When he said it like that, it sounded terrible. Was I really that snobby? I hadn't known anything back then. How you looked and the car your parent's drove had been all that mattered. I'd changed since then. He had to know that.

"I'm sorry," I said. I met his gaze and held it for a moment. I really hoped he saw how true those words were.

He shrugged. "No big deal. I'm happy you enjoyed my family."

I steadied the chair as I watched him. Suddenly, I didn't want to be on this side of the room. Right now, he felt a million miles away. I stood and walked over to his bed, flopping down next to him.

He laughed and pulled me close. He kissed my cheek.

I sat cross-legged so I could study him. "My life is falling apart," I told him. It felt good to confess that. He was the only person I wanted to know what was happening to me. The only person I felt I could be vulnerable with.

He nodded as he cradled my cheek with his hand and leaned forward to kiss my nose. When he pulled back, he rested his forehead on mine.

"Wanna know what I wished for?" he asked me.

I widened my eyes as I studied him. "But it won't come true," I whispered.

He shrugged as he pressed his lips to mine. When he pulled back, he smiled. "It already has."

CHAPTER SEVENTEEN

I stayed in Cade's room until his mom came in and told us that it was time for me to go home. I didn't want to leave, but I knew I'd overstayed my welcome. Cade started to protest, but I shook my head and said it was fine.

I grabbed my purse and shoes and followed Cade out to his motorcycle. I reveled in the feeling of being pressed next to him as he sped down the street. The wind whipped around us and I actually felt happy for a moment.

There was nothing else I needed. No amount of money or parental acceptance would make me as happy as I felt with Cade. He was my person. As crazy and strange as that was to admit, it was true.

I squeezed my arm as I thought about the last few days. What a whirlwind. But I wouldn't change anything.

Well, maybe the breakdown of my family, but that was it. Everything else had been perfect.

When we got to my car, the diner had closed. It's neon lighting surrounded us as Cade pulled me up onto the hood of my van and kissed me. He took my breath away. I lost myself in the feeling of him pressed against me.

When we finally came up for air, he smiled at me. "I should go, Chocolate Milk."

My lips felt puffy and my gaze was hazy. I smiled and nodded. "Yeah, you should."

He leaned forward and pressed featherlight kisses to my cheeks and lips. "I don't want to."

I giggled. "I get that," I said as I wrapped my arms around him, pulling him closer.

He groaned. "That's not helping."

"That was the plan," I whispered in his ear.

He kissed me again, this time harder, like he wanted to make sure I understood just what I was doing to him. I responded with just as much feeling.

When we broke apart, he growled. "I have to go. Now."

I pressed my lips with my fingertips and nodded. "Okay."

He grabbed my hand and kissed it. "I'll see you tomorrow?"

I nodded. "Of course."

He winked at me as he turned and got onto his bike. He waited until I got into my car and started it before he peeled out. I sat back, watching him until he disappeared around the corner. Butterflies swarmed my stomach as I pushed my car into drive and headed down the street. The street that would lead me to my house.

I sighed as I tried to hang onto the lingering feeling of completeness. But the farther I got from Cade, the faster they faded. I didn't want to go back. Home didn't feel like home anymore. It was just a place where I lived.

When I pulled into the driveway, I glanced up at the towering two-story building. A few lights were on here and there, but that was it. I doubted anyone was even home.

I killed the engine and got out. I strung my purse onto my shoulder and pulled open the back door. When I entered the kitchen, I stopped. Dad was standing at the counter, writing on a pad of paper. His pen hovered above it as he turned his attention over to me.

An unsure expression passed over his face. He must have seen my reaction. I *hated* him.

"Hey, Pen," he said, giving me a weary smile.

I fought the urge to call him all the names that were swarming in my head. "What are you doing here?" I narrowed my eyes. "Don't you have a new family to get to?"

His eyebrows shot up as a stunned look settled on his features. "What makes you say that?"

I rolled my eyes as I walked past him, setting my purse on the counter. "I saw you," I said. Dad sputtered a few times. I didn't allow him to continue. "You're a terrible person," I said, cursing myself for the fact that my voice cracked. I wasn't supposed to care. He was the one leaving, not me.

"Pen, you don't understand."

Tears stung my eyes at his lame attempt to justify himself. "I don't have to. You cheated. You're the one leaving." I turned and pointed to the door. "Just go."

He followed my gesture with his gaze and then turned around to study me. I could see all the things he wanted to say settled in his eyes. But, he didn't say anything. Instead, he nodded, finished scribbling something on the paper, grabbed his suitcase, and walked out the door.

When he left, the sob that I had been holding in exploded from my body and I crumpled to the floor. My heart broke into a million pieces as I cried there on the hard tile. I'd never stood up to him or Mom like that. I was shaking.

I grabbed a dish towel that was hanging from the oven door and used it to wipe my tears. Finally, when I no longer had any energy, I took a deep breath. I was exhausted, but I felt better.

I grabbed the side of the counter and pulled myself up. After a huge glass of water, I felt less dehydrated and more clear headed. So much so, that I felt completely ridiculous for spending the last fifteen minutes crying on the kitchen floor. What was the matter with me? Why was I acting like such a baby about this?

I let out my breath slowly as I reached over to grab my phone from my purse. When I passed by the piece of paper that Dad had been writing on, I paused.

Pen and Pat,

If you need me, here's my new address.

Come by any time.

Love, Dad

I stared at the address. It was about fifteen minutes from here. In one of the newer developments.

I read the address a few times. His address. The one he'd left us for.

All I wanted to do was drive there and see the place he now called home. Was it nice? Was it bigger than the one we lived in as a family?

I grabbed my purse and shoved my phone back into it. I picked up the paper and pushed through the back door. I didn't want to lose my resolve.

Once I was in the driver's seat, I found my keys and started the engine. I typed the address into my phone and followed the monotone directions fifteen minutes down the road. As I pulled into the community that Dad now lived in, I swallowed.

The houses were two times the size of ours. I felt dwarfed as I drove through the neighborhood. The lawns were manicured. Some houses were guarded by gates. It was definitely over Dad's salary. Which meant one thing. His new girlfriend was rich.

A painful feeling settled in my gut. He was leaving us for a wealthy woman? I'd always figured my parents cared about how we were perceived, but this? Leaving us because he felt we were too poor? That was a new low.

Google Maps informed me that I had *arrived* as I

pulled past a huge, white three-story house. It had a double entry door that opened outward. A few large windows were lit up. A fountain bubbled in the circular driveway.

How was this where Dad was now living?

I leaned forward, over the steering wheel, so I could see the house in its entirety. Who lived here? I didn't even know houses like this existed in our town.

I wanted to throw up. Dad had sold out. He took a fancy life with lots of money in the bank over his family. We were nothing to him. And the note he left?

It was a pity note. I'm sure he felt guilty for abandoning us, so he wrote that he loved us to make himself feel better. I crumbled it up and threw it onto the floor. And I'd fallen for it.

How could I be so stupid?

Before the few remaining pieces of my heart shattered again, I found my phone and called Cade.

Ten rings later, I got his voicemail.

I closed my eyes as I let the familiarity of his voice wash over me. I swallowed when the beep came.

"Hey, Cade. It's me. You're probably sleeping right now." I sighed. Sleeping sounded amazing. I was exhausted. "I got home and my dad was there. He was writing a note to me and Patricia. He said he loved us and that we could visit him."

I shifted in my seat as I recalled our fight. "I, of course, told him to get out. He did. Then, I felt guilty. I'm so stupid," I muttered under my breath. "I decided to come to his new house to apologize."

I leaned my head back onto the headrest. "Get this, he lives in a mansion community just off of 479. Looks like good ole' dad is moving up." I sighed. "Anyway, just wanted to talk to you. Hear your voice. I miss you." The last sentence came out barely a whisper.

I hung up and tucked my phone back into my purse. What was I doing? I was a complete and total mess. I should go home, crawl into my bed, and never come out.

I started up my van and pulled away from the mansion. I shook my head, trying to clear it, as I studied the road. I wasn't going to try to sort any of this out. I needed to stop thinking for the day.

A bit farther down the road, I drove by Mason's Grocery and More. As I studied the neon sign, I suddenly had an urge for ice cream. Cookies and Cream to be exact. I was pretty sure I'd finished the last of it a week ago, and, with everything going on, Mom hadn't been too diligent about restocking. So I flipped on my blinker and pulled into the parking lot.

I grabbed a shopping cart as I made my way into the store. Partly because I wanted something to do, and partly, because I wanted it to hold me up. I was exhausted.

I made my way to the freezer section and pulled open the door. Just as I grabbed out a gallon of Cookies and Cream, a familiar laugh filled the air around me. I glanced through the frosted door to find Tiffanii and Buddha turning down the aisle with a few of their friends.

Heat raced to my cheeks as I turned away, praying they didn't see me. There was no way I had the energy to talk to them tonight. I needed to get as far away from them as I could. Well, from Tiffanii, at least.

"Hey, Penny," Tiffanii's mocking voice said from behind me.

Too late.

I sucked in my breath, hoping that I was just dreaming all of this. But the stinging numbness that raced up my arm from the frozen ice cream told a different story. I was very much awake.

I forced a smile and turned, shutting the door behind me. "Hey, Tiffanii," I said. I prayed that my puffy, red eyes and swollen nose didn't give away the fact that I'd just been crying my eyes out.

When her gaze swept over me and I saw her eyebrows shoot up, I knew my cover had been blown. "Oh, man, have you been crying sweetheart?" she asked, wrapping her arm around my shoulders.

I shook my head as my skin crawled. "No, not crying."

She quirked her head.

She didn't believe me. And when I caught my reflection in the freezer door, I understood why. I looked like I'd had an allergic reaction while walking through the rain. I was a mess.

So I lied. "I'm having an allergic reaction. I can't eat...

shellfish." I swallowed, hoping she'd buy my lie and leave me alone.

"Oh no. Shouldn't you be at the hospital and not here, buying"—she glanced down at the gallon of ice cream I was still holding—"cookies and cream?"

I laughed, but it came out more forced than I'd hoped. I dropped the gallon bucket into my cart, and it made a rattling sound. "I was just at the doctor. He told me that ice cream is great for inflammation." I winced. Wow. My lies were getting stupider the longer I stood here.

Tiffanii tilted her head as she studied me and then turned her attention over to Buddha and his minions, who were leaning against the freezer doors, talking. "Can you guys give us a minute?"

Great. She wasn't leaving.

I guess I could just abandon my cart and take off running through the sliding doors. I'd slip into my van and drive home, where I'd disappear into my room and never come out.

As if she sensed my sudden desire to sprint like a bat out of hell, Tiffanii tightened her grip on my shoulder. "You can talk to me, Pen. We're friends."

I snorted. Just as the sound left my throat, I covered my mouth with my hand. I hadn't meant to do that. "I'm sorry," I said, hoping to cover it up.

Tiffanii pulled back and looked at me. "I get it. I come across as mean and witch-y."

I nodded. Yep. That's exactly how I would put it.

She sighed. "But that's just how I have to appear. It's my persona. Underneath it all, I'm nice." She smiled down at me. There was something genuine about her.

Was it a lie? Probably. "Ummm," I said, hesitation in my voice.

She leaned forward. "Why don't you just try me? After all"—her gaze swept up and down the aisle—"I'm the only one here. What would it hurt?"

That was true. Cade wasn't answering his phone, and if I went home, I'd be sitting in my quiet house with all these thoughts and worries clouding my mind. All I needed to do was talk. That, I could handle.

"You can trust me," she said as if she'd read my mind.

I closed my eyes and steadied my thoughts. It might be nice to talk to someone else about this. I'd dumped all my problems on Cade when he had his own to deal with. It might be good to get another person's opinion.

Before I talked myself out of it, I parted my lips, and the whole story came tumbling out. Dad. The divorce. His new girlfriend and their new home. Everything.

By the time I was finished, heat raced to my cheeks. I hadn't meant to say that much.

Tiffanii had remained quiet the whole time. She was listening intently. The expression on her face was...soft. Like she understood me.

"So I'm just trying to get over all of this and move on." I forced a smile. "It's for the best."

Tiffanii hesitated before she shook her head. "Honey, I

don't think so. You have been hurt. This woman came into your life and destroyed it. And what? She gets to go back to her fancy house with your dad?" She shook her head and raised her finger. "That woman needs to pay. She needs to know what kind of people she's screwing over."

I parted my lips to protest, but before I could say anything, she called Buddha over. I stood there, dumbly, as they spoke. Their conversation flew by me, and before I knew it, they were pushing me along with them to go buy some spray paint. Something about revenge.

What had I gotten myself into?

CHAPTER EIGHTEEN

I don't really know how I got to this point.

Somehow, I let Tiffanii convince me to buy a few bottles of red spray paint and drive with them to Dad's new house.

Now I sat inside her car as the engine idled, listening to them talk about what they were going to write. What was happening to me?

Deep down, I was terrified. What would they do to me if I didn't go along with it? Now that they knew where Dad lived, I worried that if I didn't follow through, they'd come back here and do something worse, then blame it on me.

No. The only way for this nightmare to end was to finish this and never speak to Tiffanii again.

"Hey!" Tiffanii's voice broke through my thoughts.

I turned to see her staring at me.

"You okay?" she asked, reaching out and resting her hand on my arm.

I forced a smile and nodded. "Yeah. Um-hum."

She quirked an eyebrow. "It's okay. Trust us. You'll feel better once this is all done." She shifted on her seat as she pulled out a flask and handed it over. "Wanna sip?"

Great. Now drinking was involved. I wanted to run so far here. But I couldn't, so I just shook my head. "No thanks."

She wiggled it in front of me. "You sure?"

I nodded.

"Suit yourself. More for us." After she took a few sips, she passed it around to the guys in the backseat.

My palms were sweating. Hopefully, Dad and his girl-friend would see this as a defiant teenager thing and forgive me. I just prayed that they didn't catch us.

A few minutes later—after I was pretty sure the flask was empty—everybody whooped and the car doors were thrown open. My stomach churned as I followed after them.

We snuck up the driveway. I kept my gaze trained on the windows and doors. Tiffanii and her crowd weren't exactly stealthy. Especially when they had alcohol in their systems. They kept stumbling and knocking into each other. Once they righted themselves, they would laugh while shushing the other person.

It felt like an eternity before we finally got to the garage door. We needed to get this over with as fast as possible. Tiffanii shoved a can of spray paint at me.

"We've decided to write 'Homewrecker' on the door."

She giggled and then held her finger up to my lips. "Shush," she said.

I doubted she even realized she'd been the one laughing.

Instead of correcting her, I popped off the lid and nodded. Anything to get this horrible evening over with.

I was instructed to write the letter H. I sprayed the first few lines. The paint landed on the door. It was faded and needed a few more swipes, but, as I focused on the lines, I realized that I was now defacing property. I was breaking the law.

I was *breaking the law.*

Why was I doing this? How had I let this horrible person convince me that this was okay?

I released my finger on the trigger and stepped back. I didn't want this. Sure, Dad made me mad. And his new fling? Livid. But this wasn't right. I shouldn't have allowed Tiffanii and her crew to manipulate me.

"Guys, wait," I said, holding up my hand. "This isn't right."

Everyone stopped and turned to look at me. Their eyes were wide as they studied me.

And then Tiffanii stepped into view. Her jovial expression had turned to anger.

"What?" she spat.

"I don't think that we should be doing this," I said, my voice growing quieter the closer she got. My stomach dropped as she approached me.

"I knew it," she said. The look in her eye sent shivers down my back. It was full of anger and hatred.

"But—"

She held up her finger. Her lips pursed as she turned her gaze toward the ground as if she were trying to compose herself. "You act all tough. Pretend that you deserve Cade. But in the end, you're just a stuck-up rich girl who throws tantrums." She leaned closer to me. "Oh, I'm so sorry that your parents split up. Boo hoo. Rich girl didn't get what she wanted." She shoved my shoulder, causing me to stumble backwards. Luckily, I caught myself before I fell over.

"You're wrong," I said, narrowing my eyes.

She placed her hand on her chest dramatically. "Oh, no. I'm wrong? What ever will I do?" She fanned herself with her hand.

This night was sinking faster than the Titanic. I needed to get them to leave. Now.

"I think you should leave," I said, stepping up to her.

Her eyes widened as she studied me. "Wow. Rich girl's got some big-girl panties." She glanced over at her friends. They were waiting for her commands. "Finish up, guys," she said. Then she turned to me. "Then we'll be out of your hair."

I grabbed onto my purse and moved closer to the garage. There was only one thing that I could do. I needed to call the police. They weren't going to leave, and I doubted the vandalism would stop at the spray paint. I did not want to see what they were capable of.

When Tiffanii wasn't looking, I grabbed my phone and dialed 911. Tipping my head, I raised the phone to my cheek and waited as the ringing tone filled my ear.

"911, can I get your name and address?" the dispatcher asked.

I lowered my voice as far as it could go and still be heard. "I need some help. There are kids at a house vandalizing it."

"Okay. What's your address?"

I closed my eyes, trying to see the piece of paper and recall what my dad had written on it. I rattled it off, hoping I didn't get a number confused.

"I will send a patrol car there to check it out," she said after she read the address back to me.

"Thanks," I said and pulled my phone from my cheek. Just as I turned back to the group, Tiffanii came into view.

"Whatcha doing?" she asked, grabbing my phone from my hand. "You snitched?" Her gaze met mine as she rolled her eyes. "What a dork." She motioned to the people behind her. "Come on, guys. I guess our damsel in distress isn't loving us anymore. Let's get out of here."

They all nodded, dropped the spray paint, and made their way to her car.

She clicked her tongue, drawing my attention back over to her. "What a disappointment, rich girl. And I thought we could be friends."

I glared at her. Deep down, I hated her. She'd exploited me. Took advantage of the fact that I felt vulnerable. What a horrible person. "We will never be friends."

She widened her eyes in a mocking manner. Then she raised her hands and backed away. "Wow. Don't break my heart," she said, clutching her chest.

"Leave. Now."

She gave me one last grin and a wink, then turned and left. After she slipped into the driver's seat, she started the engine and pulled away.

And I was left alone. With a half-spray-painted garage door.

I sighed as I picked up the cans of spray paint and piled them together.

"Pen? What's going on?"

My heart sank at the sound of Cade's voice. It had to be a dream. Or in this situation, a nightmare.

I turned to see him standing there with a confused expression on his face. I parted my lips. I wanted to say something, I really did. But no words came.

"What did you do?" he asked, turning to study the half-finished graffiti. HO WREC was written across the white garage door.

"It wasn't me," I finally managed. And then I shook my head. That wasn't true. I was the stupid person who had allowed Tiffanii into my life and brought her here. "I mean, it was me."

He pointed toward the letters. "You did this?" Then he furrowed his brow. "Why?"

I shrugged. "I was angry."

He shoved his hands into his front pockets. "I just don't

understand." He leaned over and picked up a spray can. As he turned it over, he quickly set it back down on the ground. Apparently, there had been some paint on the outside, and now he had it all over his fingertips.

I stared at him as he rubbed his fingers together.

"I know." I didn't know how to explain this. Did I tell him about Tiffanii? It felt a little like I would be justifying my actions by blaming someone else. Truth was, I'd allowed her to manipulate me. And then my stomach heaved as the realization that Cade was here hit me.

He was a great guy. He'd heard my distressed voicemail and came here to comfort me. I swallowed against the lump in my throat. I was the worst person ever. I didn't deserve him. Here I was, with my life in complete shambles. The only thing that I could do was drag him down with me.

He needed to get as far away from me as possible. I forced a steady look as I met his gaze. Mustering all the strength I could, I parted my lips and said the four words that I knew were going to shatter my heart, "You need to go."

He raised his eyebrows as he studied me. "What?"

Bile rose up in my throat, but I had to push on. "You need to go. You don't belong here. We're done." I swallowed. "This is what happens when I get involved with someone. You've rubbed off on me." Ouch. Those words were squeezing my chest. Why was I saying these things?

His eyes narrowed. "You're saying you did this because you're involved with me?"

I nodded, fighting back the tears that brimmed on my

lids. "Why else would I do this? You've influenced me. I was a good kid. Straight-A student before we became"—I waved my hand at him—"whatever it is we became."

He took a step back. "What are you doing? Are you breaking up with me?"

I steadied my gaze, hoping I wouldn't break down in the middle of this. "Yes. You need to leave. The last thing I should have ever done was agree to help you." I turned, wrapping my arms around my chest. "We're done."

From the corner of my eye, I saw Cade study me and then turn and make his way down the driveway. Not wanting to stand there alone, I ducked my head and made my way around the house, where I could hide.

I was such a mess. My life was such a mess. How could it have come to this?

Cade was gone. Because I forced him out.

My parents were split, and I was literally standing in the backyard of Dad's mistress's house.

How was I ever going to come back from this?

Just as I passed the back of the garage, a flood light clicked on. I blinked as its brightness blinded me. Spots clouded my vision as I rubbed my eyes.

The sound of a door opening caused my heart to pick up speed.

"Penny?" Dad's deep voice asked.

I chewed my lip as I turned to him and nodded.

He stepped out onto the deck and pulled the door closed

behind him. I tried to ignore the fact that he was wearing his pajamas. Just like he did at home, before this all happened.

"What are you doing here?"

I shrugged. I didn't want to tell him that I'd brought a group of delinquents here to deface his new girlfriend's garage door. Or that I was stalking him. Or that I came here to find out who he'd replaced us with. "You left the address, and I wanted to see what you traded us for." I winced at the bite in my tone. Man, I needed to get home and go to bed.

He folded his arms over his chest as he studied me. "Okay," he said.

Not knowing what to do, I turned away. I didn't want to be here right now. I needed to get home, take a shower, and go to bed. Too bad I had a thirty-minute walk back to the store to get my car.

"Do you need a ride home?" Dad asked.

I just waved away his question. At least with the walk, I'd have some quiet time. I'd be able to think, to process my thoughts, and decide what I was going to do.

CHAPTER NINETEEN

The rest of the weekend sucked.

Lucky for me, Mom and Patricia didn't bother me, and Dad didn't come around.

I spent all of Sunday in bed, eating Pop-Tarts and watching ridiculous Hallmark movies. Anything to drown out the aching hole that was left in my heart from Cade's absence.

How had I grown so accustomed to him being around? We'd only just started tolerating each other. Why couldn't I go back to hating him as much as I did before? Back when life was simple.

As I buried myself under my covers Monday morning, I knew why. Because I'd seen the side of Cade that I never knew existed. The kind, loving, smart, and incredibly sexy side of him. And I missed all of that. He'd changed me, and I was never going to be the same.

My alarm rang again. I groaned and flung the comforter off of me. I needed to get ready for school. I'd already completely screwed up my personal life. I couldn't let my grades slip—even though the thought of going to school made me want to puke.

I sighed. Too bad I couldn't live in my bed forever.

After a long shower, I got dressed in a t-shirt and jeans. I threw my wet hair up into a bun and grabbed my backpack. I tried to ignore the fact that I hadn't done any of my homework all weekend. I was going to have some explaining to do when I got to school.

And then my stomach churned.

I was going to see Cade in a few short hours. Cade.

My heart squeezed as tears formed on my lids. I missed him.

I cleared my throat as I walked down the stairs. I couldn't think about him anymore. We were done. I was completely wrong for him. We'd tried to make it work, and it didn't. It was time that I started accepting that.

Or, at least, force it from my mind so it didn't break my heart every time I thought about it.

I ate breakfast solo and then headed out the door. Mom and Patricia seemed to be avoiding the house as much as I had. I wasn't even sure when I'd seen them last. What a strange turn our life had taken.

When I got to school, I texted Crista. I didn't want to be alone today. I needed my best friend.

She responded right away: she was sitting at a lunch

table, waiting for the bell to ring. I made a beeline for the lunch room. Just as I turned the corner, I ran into someone.

He humphed and wrapped a hand around my arm to help steady me.

"Sorry," Cade said.

Of course. Out of the 700 students here, I had to run into Cade. I cursed fate's cruel humor.

"It's okay," I whispered as I met his gaze. I couldn't help it. I was like a moth to flame.

He raised his eyebrows and he dropped his hand as if he'd been burned. He reached up to run his hand through his hair.

The silence around us suffocated me. I had to say something.

"Cade, I—"

He held up his hand. "I think you've done enough," he said as he stepped to the side and disappeared into the crowd.

A tear slipped down my cheek as I ducked my head and slipped into the bathroom. I found an empty stall and collapsed against the wall.

The tears fell more freely now. My heart was breaking in my chest, and there was nothing I could do to stop it. It was all my fault. As much as I wanted to blame someone else for my pain, I couldn't. I'd been the idiot who ruined everything.

The warning bell rang, so I grabbed some toilet paper

and dried my eyes. I took a few deep breaths and then opened the door.

Just my luck, Tiffanii and a few of her posse members were standing in front of the bathroom mirror, applying eyeliner to their already overly lined lids.

When her gaze fell on me, a sick smile spread across her lips. "Well, if it isn't rich girl," she said, turning to face me.

I glared at her as I threaded my thumbs through my backpack straps and headed toward the door.

"Whoa, hang on," she said, grabbing my arm and pulling me to a stop.

"Let go of me," I said, glaring over at her.

Her eyes widened as she dropped her hand. "Fine," she said.

I didn't wait for her to continue. I focused on the exit. There was nothing that was going to stop me from leaving.

"I thought you might want some information about Cade," she called after me.

Except that.

I stopped and turned toward her. "What?"

She smiled and leaned against the sink. She'd gotten my attention, and that made her happy. I didn't know it was possible to hate her more.

She folded her arms. "I thought you might want to know about Cade," she repeated.

I groaned. I didn't want to play her games, but if she had information about him, I needed to know. Like, my body wasn't going to do anything I told it to do until she spilled. "Okay. What do I need to know?"

She grinned. "Oh, something about him getting arrested on Saturday."

I stared at her. "What?"

"Apparently, the cops you called on us stopped him. They found spray paint all over his hands, and another source told them that they saw him vandalizing the house..." She sucked the air in through her teeth as she tapped her chest. "It didn't look good for good ole' Cade."

My stomach plummeted. My ears rang. My heart galloped in my chest. "He was arrested because of you?"

Her smile spread across her face. "Oh yeah. And he's in deep—" Her eyes widened as Mrs. Sanchez, the art teacher, walked into the bathroom. "Crap," she said as Mrs. Sanchez shot her a pointed look.

"What are you ladies doing in here? The warning bell rang. You should be headed to class." She pointed her finger at us and then disappeared into a stall.

Taking this as my opportunity to leave, I turned and slipped into the hallway.

Everything seemed to be moving in slow motion. I'd gotten Cade arrested? He must hate me. Here he was, trying to put his life on the right path, and I went and screwed it up for him. I was such an idiot.

I slipped into Ceramics and tried to keep from looking to see where Cade was. But, my stupid body wouldn't listen to me, so I spotted him a few seconds later. He was sitting in the back with his head down. His Calc book was open in front of him, and he was writing something down in his notebook.

I stared at him as I walked to my seat. Inside my head, I was begging him to look at me. I needed him to know that I hadn't meant for that to happen. It was completely my fault, and I was going to fix it.

But he stayed focused on his homework until the bell rang. Mr. Meyer stood in front of the class and informed us of the new project we'd be working on in groups. I secretly hoped I'd be paired with Cade, but no such luck. Instead, I got stuck with chatty Caroline, who didn't stop talking until the bell rang.

I gathered my things as fast as I could and shoved them into my backpack. I had an hour of Economics and then Calculus. If I wanted to talk to Cade, I needed to corner him now.

Thankfully, he wasn't in as much of a rush as I was. I made it out of the classroom and into the hall before him. So I stood next to the door, waiting. I felt a bit like a lioness waiting to pounce. But, when I saw him, my heart rate went galloping off, and it was all I could do to reach out and grab his arm.

"Wait!" I said, too loud. I mentally slapped myself.

Get a grip.

I loosened my grasp. "I mean, can we talk?"

Cade's gaze moved from my hand up to my face. His

expression was a mix of hurt and anger. "What do you want, Penelope?"

I nodded toward the far alcove. He allowed me to lead him over to it. Once we were out of the throng of people, my throat went dry. Why did I decide that this was a good idea?

When I didn't speak, his eyebrows went up. "If you don't have anything to say, I should go. I've got class to get to." He pulled the strap of his backpack up onto his shoulder.

"I'm sorry," I whispered. Why had I all of a sudden become mute? I had him. He was willing to listen to me. And yet, words wouldn't form in my mind.

"You're sorry?" He sighed. "For what?"

Tears formed on my lids again. Blast these stupid emotions. I swear, before this week, I'd cried about five times, total. Now? It seemed I was tearing up every five minutes.

I shook my head. I could be strong. "For this weekend."

He snorted, but the pain was written all over his face. "It's okay. I'm used to getting screwed over." He met my gaze again, and I could see the wall he'd put up between us.

I'd hurt him. Bad.

He turned and stepped toward the hall. "I should go. If that's all you wanted, then you did what you needed to do." He hesitated as he looked over at me again. "I hope you feel better now."

And with that, he slipped into the crowd and disappeared.

I was alone. Again.

I covered my mouth with my hand as a sob escaped my lips. What had I done? How had I become this person? I was horrible and I'd treated Cade even worse. He didn't deserve just my apology, I needed to fix this. I'd made a mess of my life, and he'd been the one to suffer because of it.

I allowed myself a minute to compose myself before I forced the tears to stop. Once I'd contained my emotions, I shouldered my backpack and stepped out into the hallway. After school, I was going to make this right. I was going to fix the things that I'd broken.

I could do this.

CHAPTER TWENTY

After school, I met up with Crista. I needed to apologize to her for not meeting her this morning—and get her advice. I needed to run things by the people who knew and loved me. I'd made too many mistakes over the past week, and I doubted my ability to make good, rational decisions.

I walked out of school and over to my car. Crista had agreed to ride home with me. I was grateful that it gave us more time to chat.

Crista was standing next to my car with her blue hair sticking up all over the place. She had her ear buds in and was bobbing her head to whatever was playing. When I approached, I threw my arms around her and hugged her.

She laughed. "Whoa, Pen. What's going on?" she asked.

I looked up at her. My expression must have said it all because her brow furrowed. "You okay?" she asked.

I shook my head as I walked over to the driver's side and

opened the door. She climbed in, and I started the engine. As soon as we were on the road, I parted my lips and the entire story spilled out.

By the time I was finished, I'd parked in front of my house. Crista had remained quiet the entire time. I was hoping that was because she was listening and not because she'd suddenly realized how crazy her best friend was and was rapidly rethinking our relationship.

I snuck a peek over at her. She had a contemplative look on her face. I winced as I asked, "So, what do you think?"

And then she laughed. Like a full belly, loud as heck, laugh. I stared at her. What was happening? I replayed what I'd told her in my mind and couldn't find where any of it was this hilarious.

The only conclusion I could draw was that I'd shocked my best friend so much that she'd officially snapped.

Her laughter died down to a chuckle. She wiped at her eyes as she glanced over at me. "Oh, Penny. Sweet, naive, Penny."

My eyes widened. Why was she talking to me like I was a kid?

She reached over and patted my hand. "Your innate desire to please people has come back to bite you on the butt." She grinned at me.

"What are you talking about?"

She sighed. "I've known you your whole life, and you've spent every minute trying to please everyone. When you've finally found yourself unable to please anyone, you snapped." She patted my knee. "It's good to see that you're not a robot." Then her expression grew serious. "Cade was good for you."

The sound of Cade's name made my heart squeeze. Also, the word "was." Cade "was" good for me. He was in my past, even though I so desperately wanted him to be my future.

I let out a breath as I leaned my head against the seat. "So what do I do?"

Crista tapped her chin. "Let me find out more about Cade. You"—she pointed toward me—"talk to your dad. If the police are involved, I have a feeling that he pressed charges. If you talk to your dad, maybe he'll drop them." She shrugged

It was worth a shot.

I nodded. Good. That was something I could do. Why hadn't I thought of that before? We both got on our phones. I was texting Dad and she was texting someone who might know about Cade.

Soon, our phones were chiming with messages. Dad agreed to meet me at his new house for dinner while Stephanie, the school's gossip, told Crista that Cade had a hearing on Wednesday.

That meant I had two days to fix this mess.

————

THAT EVENING, I pulled up to Dad's new house. I killed the engine as I stared at the garage. Someone had tried to scrub the words off of the door but hadn't been successful. I could still see the faded letters.

Acid rose up in my throat. How was I going to do this? I didn't want to walk into Dad's new house and ask for forgiveness. He hurt me. He hurt our family.

Just as my anger bubbled to the surface, I pushed it down. I was doing this for Cade. I was going to fix this.

I pulled my keys from the ignition and threw them into my purse. I opened the car door and stepped out. I took a deep breath and made my way up to the front stoop. I stared at the dark wood door with a lion's head knocker.

This was it. I was going to meet my new...whatever she was.

I steeled my emotions as I raised my hand and rang the doorbell. I could hear it chime on the other side.

A few seconds later, the door opened, and I was met with the woman I'd seen kissing Dad a few days ago. She was short with dark skin and black hair. Her eyes widened as a slow smile spread across her lips.

"You must be Penelope," she said.

I tried not to glare, I really did. But the thought that this woman was the reason we were no longer a family flooded my mind. Instead of talking, I just nodded.

She seemed to understand my reaction because she didn't press me. Instead, she stepped aside and waved to the foyer. "Come on in. Your dad's setting the table."

Ugh. I was actually going to have to eat here.

I managed a small, "Thank you" as I followed after her.

We entered an enormous dining room, where Dad was setting the utensils next to the plates. When he saw me, he smiled.

"Hey, Pen. I'm glad you could make it," he said as he straightened and came around to hug me.

I stiffened. I wasn't ready for that kind of physical contact just yet. Sure, I was here to apologize and take ownership for what I did. But I definitely wasn't here to forgive Dad or his new girlfriend. That was a whole other wound that still needed to heal.

Dad noticed my reaction. He pulled away and pushed his hand through his hair. "I'm making lasagna. I know it's your favorite. Why don't you have a seat, and I'll grab it." He glanced over to his girlfriend. "Want to help me, Jenny?"

Oh, so her name was Jenny. Lovely.

As they left the room, I slipped onto the seat that he'd motioned toward. I was grateful for some privacy. When I was alone, I didn't have to pretend that everything was okay. I should be able to show my real feelings about what they'd done to our family. I didn't have to fake a smile.

I closed my eyes as I refocused my thoughts. I just needed to get through this dinner and then I could get as far away from this place as possible. Distance and time were the only things that could heal me from what my parents had done. And there was no forcing it to make it go faster.

When they returned, Jenny set a bowl of garlic

bread next to the bowl of salad, and Dad set a steaming pan of lasagna in the center. We dished it up and ate in silence. Their occasional glances to each other weren't lost on me. They were anything but subtle.

After I cleaned my plate, I set my fork down and turned to them. I was ready to get this over with.

"I was the one who spray painted your garage."

Dad's eyebrows rose. "What?" he asked.

I took a deep breath. "I was the one who spray painted the garage," I repeated.

"No, honey. It wasn't you. It was a boy," Jenny said, resting her hand on the table in front of her.

I shook my head. When she talked, my skin crawled. I stilled my frustration and turned back to them. This wasn't the time to get all smart-alecky on them.

"It was me. I came here on Saturday to apologize for how I treated you, Dad." My voice grew quieter with each word. I cleared my throat. "But when I saw what you replaced us with, I got angry. I drove to the grocery store to get some ice cream and that's..." Was I going to tell them about Tiffanii? I decided not to. It had been my decision, and I needed to own up to all of it. "That's where I found the spray paint. I came back here, and Cade showed up. He's...a good friend."

Dad kept quiet, studying me. So I continued.

"He told me to stop, and I told him to go home. He left, and I went around the house. That's when you saw me. I guess some cops were close by and they caught him. They were lied to and assumed that he did it."

Dad stood and began to pace next to the table. "Why would you do this?" he asked.

"Ted," Jenny said. She turned to look at him. They had another one of their non-verbal stare downs.

Not wanting to stick around and have them talk about me, without really talking about me, I stood. "I need you to drop the charges against Cade. It wasn't his fault. He was doing the right thing." I met Jenny's gaze.

She studied me for a moment before she nodded. "I'll talk to my lawyer."

That was all I needed to hear. I'd done my job, now I could leave. I gave her a quick smile as I headed toward the front door.

"Hey, Penny? Wait," she called after me.

I fought it, but I stopped and turned to see her behind me.

"Thanks for being honest. I know with everything going on, you probably hate me." She sighed as she wrung her hands. "I hope we can move past all of this in the future."

Not likely, but I wasn't going to say that when I needed her to help Cade. "Yeah, maybe," I said as I turned the door handle and stepped outside.

Just as I got into my car, Dad caught the door.

"Penny," he said.

I hesitated and glanced up. "What?"

I saw his jaw clench. He probably wasn't happy with the

way I was talking to him, but he'd hurt me, and a wound like that took time to heal. Then his face softened.

"Thanks for telling the truth, but don't think you won't be punished for that," he said, nodding toward the garage door.

I glanced over and then turned back to him. "Sounds fair." I started the engine. Sure, I wasn't happy with him, but that didn't mean there wasn't going to be a consequence for what I'd done. I'd made a mistake, and I was okay with fixing it.

I'd deal with Dad and his stupid mistakes later.

Dad looked stunned. I was pretty sure he was expecting more of a fight from me.

"I should probably go," I said, wiggling the door.

Dad nodded and took a step back. I shut my door and backed out of the driveway.

Well, I'd fixed one problem—on to the next. Nervousness rose up in my stomach. This next one was too important. What if I messed it up?

I swallowed. I couldn't think like that. Even if, at the end of all of this, Cade hated me, it didn't matter. I would make it right, and what ever else happened, happened.

CHAPTER TWENTY-ONE

Wednesday came faster that I'd anticipated.

School flew by, and, before I knew it, I was standing in my bathroom, staring at my reflection. My hair was pulled back into a bun at the base of my neck. I'd grabbed my suit I bought for debate last year. I hoped it would help me look more presentable.

I was going into a courtroom. I needed to look clean and professional. I was going to plead Cade's case.

I glanced down at my phone, which had just chimed. Crista texted me that she was outside. Thankfully, my friend had agreed to join me on this crazy crusade. I was grateful to have her by my side.

I wasn't sure what Cade was going to do when I crashed his hearing, but I was pretty sure he wasn't going to be happy. He'd avoided me every time I saw him. When I tried to approach him, he had turned the other way.

Which was why I was glad to be speaking up in court. He literally couldn't leave. He'd have to stay there and hear what I had to say. It was perfect.

I grabbed my phone and purse and headed out of my room. I passed by the kitchen where Mom was sitting at the counter. She was eating a muffin and shuffling through the mail. I'd come clean after I got back from Dad's yesterday. She wasn't happy, but I think my parents were cutting me some slack lately because of the bomb they dropped on me.

I was grateful for that.

"Heading to the courthouse?" she called after me.

I paused and turned to face her. "Yeah." I gave her a worried look. "I hope he forgives me."

Mom slipped off the stool and walked over to give me a hug. "He will, honey. You're a good girl. If he can't see what a catch you are, then he's blind." She pulled back to give me a kiss on my cheek.

I smiled at her. Worry flitted in my stomach. "Thanks. Are you doing okay?" After I had confessed everything to her, we talked for a while about Dad and Jenny. She admitted that it hurt, but that she'd done some stupid things in the marriage as well.

I learned a lot more than I wanted to about Mom. Something about an emotional affair. None of it made me feel better, but it did help me see that perhaps splitting ways was really for the best. If I wanted my parents to be happy, I had to accept their decision.

I told her it would take me time to get used to it, and she agreed, telling me that she was here to help me.

All in all, I had a healthy conversation with both of my parents. There was no fighting. No name calling. Just two people talking. And even though it hurt me more than anything to say the words *divorce* and *separate lives,* I realized we were still a family. Nothing was going to change that.

Mom nodded as she pulled back to walk over to the cupboard and fill a cup with water. Once she was done, she set it next to the sink. "I'll be fine, sweetie," she said, smiling at me.

I could see the pain in her expression, even though she was trying to cover it up. I guess it was going to take some time for all of us to heal.

I studied her. "You sure?"

She nodded and waved toward the door. "Go. Fix this with Cade."

I glanced at the door, and my stomach churned. I'd been waiting all week to do this, and, suddenly, I was scared. What if he ignored me? What if it didn't change anything with the judge? What if it didn't change anything with us?

I wasn't sure how I'd come back from something like that.

Deciding that wallowing in the what-ifs wasn't going to help, I tried to think positive. I plastered a smile on my face and marched out the door.

When I plopped into Crista's front seat, she glanced over at me. "What's with you?"

I looked over at her. "What?"

"You're grinning like a ventriloquist doll." She shuddered. "You look creepy."

I softened my smile and rubbed my cheeks. It actually hurt to force that smile. "Sorry. I'm just nervous."

She nodded as she pulled out of the drive. "I get that. But you have nothing to be worried about. Things will work out. Cade's going to forgive you." She paused to stare at me directly. "That boy loves you. I've never seen someone stare so intently at another person in my life." She nodded again as she focused on the road. "He loves you," she repeated.

I wanted to shush her words. I was worried they would jinx us, or something.

She drove to the courthouse, and I sat there, listening to her talk about her classes and Peter, the guy she was desperately in love with, but who didn't even know she existed. By the time she pulled into the parking lot and killed the engine, I was pretty sure I was going to have a panic attack.

I glanced over at her. "I can't do this."

Crista reached out and squeezed my hand. "You can. Like I said—"

"He loves me," I whispered. I wished I could believe her words. But she hadn't seen his face when he told me to leave him alone. I'd never seen someone so hurt and angry before. I was sure if he could have turned me into a pillar of salt right there, he would have.

"Besides, I drove you all the way here. I want to see how this turns out." She grinned at me as she unbuckled her seatbelt and pulled open her door.

I groaned. Great. My life had become a soap opera for my best friend.

Bolstering myself up on her confidence, I followed after her. I slammed my door and took a deep breath. I could do this.

The air conditioning hit us hard as we entered the courthouse. We lived in a small town, so the building consisted of a small counter on one side and a room on the other. A few people milled around the foyer, looking bored or upset.

I let Crista lead me over to the closed doors. When we got there, she pulled on the handle, and we slipped into the room.

In front of us sat a judge. A pair of reading glasses were perched on his nose. A bailiff stood off to the side. He was leaning on his elbow that was propped up on the bench. The stenographer was reading something to the courtroom.

We slipped into the back row.

My heart picked up speed when I saw the back of Cade's head. I tried hard not to, but inside, I was willing him to turn around. I wanted him to see that I was here. That I was going to make all of this go away.

"Thank you, Mrs. Nielsen," the judge said as he turned to Cade. "Now that we got the notes from last time, let's discuss why we are here." He cleared his throat as he shuffled some papers on his desk. "So, Mr. Kelley, want to tell me why you are here?"

I saw Cade move to speak, but I couldn't let him. There was no way I was going to sit here and let him take the fall for me.

I stood, raising my hand. "Your honor?"

The judge stopped and turned to stare at me. The few people that dotted the room turned as well. When Cade's gaze landed on me, I thought I would faint on the spot. His eyebrows shot up as he studied me.

"Yes?" the judge asked.

Taking that as my cue to keep going, I pushed past Crista and made my way to the front. I glanced around, summoning all the information I'd ever gleaned from all of the courtroom dramas Mom made me watch as a kid. "May I approach the bench?"

The judge studied me. "What did you want to say?"

I cleared my throat. "I have new evidence." Was that the right thing to say?

The judge stared at me from above his readers. "You do know that the people dropped the charges."

Relief flooded my chest. Good. Well, at least Jenny kept her word. That was nice.

"Yes. But this is more to the character of Cade." I winced at the feeling of his name rolling off my tongue. I missed him so much. I was pretty sure there was a Cade-sized hole in my heart.

The judge raised his eyebrows and leaned back on his chair. "All right. If you feel it's important." He waved to the seat next to him. "Why don't you join me up here?"

I swallowed as I moved to sit. On one hand, my knees were about to give out, so sitting was a smart option. On the other hand, sitting here put me right in front of Cade. As I brought my gaze up, I saw him staring at the tabletop.

I gathered my strength and started.

"None of what happened to that garage was Cade's fault." I fiddled with the hem of my suit jacket. "It was all my fault." I let my voice trail off. "Everything."

That seemed to get Cade's attention. He glanced up at me, and his brows furrowed.

"So he didn't vandalize that house?"

I turned back to the judge and shook my head. "It was me. I take responsibility for it all. I was upset and allowed some other kids to talk me into bringing them there. I took my anger out in the wrong way. Cade was there to stop me. He..." I closed my eyes for a moment as I allowed the memories we'd shared together this past week wash over me. "He was trying to help me."

When the judge didn't respond, I continued.

"Cade is the best person I know. He is kind. He is sweet. He is considerate. He loves his family, even though they've hurt and disappointed him." I glanced back at his mom and grandmother, who were sitting behind him. "It's a trait that I could learn."

When my gaze fell on Cade, I saw that his expression hadn't changed. He looked as if he wasn't sure how to process what I was saying. But I was on a roll, so I wasn't going to stop.

"I used to hate Cade. But as I got to know him, I learned that there is so much about him that I..." I hesitated. Did I want to say it? Yes, I did. Cade had to know. "That I love." Tears filled my eyes. "He's my best friend." I laughed as I glanced up to the ceiling. "Oh, wow. It feels so weird to say that. For so long, he was my enemy."

I glanced over to the judge, who was watching me. "And I have you to thank."

"Me?" the judge asked.

I nodded. "You forced him to be better. My principal asked me to help him. So, if it wasn't for you, I'd still hate him." I dabbed at my eyes. "Please don't punish him for what I did. Cade's a good guy. The world needs him in it." I turned my attention back to Cade and let all the feelings that had bubbled up inside of me rest in my gaze. I wanted him to know that what I said was true. He meant so much to me.

And I couldn't lose him.

When the judge realized that I was done, he excused me from the stand.

I went back and collapsed next to Crista. She hugged me and told me that my confession was "daytime-television worthy." I just nodded, trying to calm my shaking body.

The rest of the session went by in a blur. The judge talked to Cade and told him he was disappointed, but happy to hear that he was turning his life around. Instead of any legal action, he was going to sentence him to community service. Cade accepted, and the judge excused him. Then the court was no longer in session.

I stood next to Crista as Cade, his mom, and his grandmother made their way out of the room. I stared at him. Was it wrong that I'd hoped he would run into my arms and tell me that he forgave me?

He didn't, and my heart broke as he walked in front of me without acknowledging me.

I glanced back at Crista. It was too late. He hated me and would never forgive me.

She patted my back as we walked out of the courtroom. I sighed, trying to hold it together. I'd cried enough the last few days that I doubted I had anything left inside of me.

When we pulled up to my house, I opened my door.

"I'm sorry, Pen," Crista said as I stepped out.

I shrugged as I turned to lean back in. "It's okay. I tried, right?"

She nodded. "Yep. And he's a dork for not seeing how great you are."

I laughed, but it sounded as forced and fake as it felt. She waved at me as I shut the door and made my way up the walkway. Just as I stepped onto my front porch, my phone chimed.

Probably a supportive text from Crista. When I pulled

out my phone, I glanced down, and my heart nearly stopped. It was a text from Cade.

My hands shook as I swiped my phone on and read his words.

Cade: Meet me at the water tower in twenty

CHAPTER TWENTY-TWO

My whole body shook as I drove to the water tower. I feared that I'd twitch and veer off the road, where I'd crash into the trees, die, and never hear what Cade wanted to tell me.

I gripped the steering wheel tighter. There was no way I was going to heaven without talking to Cade.

As I pulled up to the water tower, I took a deep breath. Cade's bike was parked in front of me. My heartbeat picked up speed. He was here.

He was *here.*

He hadn't chickened out. He wanted to talk to me. There just might be a chance for us.

"Get a grip, Penny," I muttered under my breath. Maybe he just wanted to thank me for taking responsibility and then say goodbye forever.

That thought made my stomach twist. I blew out my

breath; I needed to stop thinking. I was going to go crazy. I just needed to turn off the engine and step out of the car, go up to the platform, and listen to what he had to say. Then, I could decide if I was going to freak out.

Silence filled my ears as I turned off the engine and slipped my keys into my purse. I opened my door and got out. When my gaze made its way up to the water tower, I found him sitting on the platform like we'd done just a few days ago.

I could see his arms resting on the bottom rail.

All I wanted to do was be up there with him. I pushed out all the built-up fear inside of me and took a deep breath. I climbed the ladder in record time. When I stood on the platform, I hesitated.

Was I ready for this?

Then Cade turned around and met my gaze, and one thought flashed through my mind.

Yes. I was ready for this.

I waited for him to do something. At first, his expression was stoic. I wasn't sure how to read it. Was he happy? Mad? Indifferent?

He turned back to the railing, and the silence that surrounded us was palpable. I was frustrated. This was ridiculous, and it was rapidly becoming apparent that this was all a ruse. He just wanted to know if he could get me here. And I came. I fell for it, hook, line, and sinker.

"This was a mistake," I said, turning and positioning

myself right on top of the ladder, preparing myself to go back down.

"I stopped by the diner before I came here."

His voice made me stop. I glanced over and studied him. "What?" I asked.

He shifted and stood. In two strides, he was next to me. Right next to me.

My breath hitched in my throat. Why was he so close? Did he know what he was doing to me?

"I went to the diner before I came here," he said again. This time, his voice was deep.

I reveled in the sound. How was I going to live without him?

"You did? Why?" I glanced up to see him staring at me. His gaze was intense.

"I needed to make a wish." It may have been my imagination, but I swear he leaned closer to me.

"And what was your wish?"

He studied me. "I thought you believed that wishes won't come true if you tell someone."

I shrugged. "You may have changed my mind."

A smile hinted on his lips. "Oh really?"

I chewed my lip as I nodded. "Yeah." Then I took a deep breath and allowed myself to be vulnerable. "You changed a lot about me. I—"

He held up his finger to silence me. "It's my turn. You had your turn earlier."

I pinched my lips together and nodded.

He pushed his hands through his hair and glanced around. An uneasy expression passed over his face as if he suddenly realized that he had the floor. I just waited. I was grateful that he decided to take charge. It took the pressure off me.

He sighed. "What you did was wrong," he said as he gave me a pointed look.

I nodded but didn't speak.

"And involving Tiffanii and her crowd?" He shook his head. "Always a big mistake."

I winced. "You found out about that?"

He nodded. "Yeah. When she approached the police while they were questioning me, I figured they had something to do with it."

That was definitely true.

He studied me. "Do you promise to never do something like that without me again?" His half smile played across his lips. "I'll be there to talk you off the ledge."

My heart began pounding. Did this mean that he forgave me? That made it sound like we had a future. Did I dare hope?

"Yes," I whispered. "I promise."

He stepped closer to me. The feeling of his warmth washed over me. It was so familiar and comforting. Even though it had only been a few days. I missed him. So much.

He raised his hand to cradle my cheek. "So, do you want to know my wish?"

I nodded as I leaned into his hand. Tears brimmed on

my cheeks as I realized what this meant. He forgave me. This nightmare was over. My chest swelled with relief.

He brushed a kiss on my cheek. "That I will never lose you like that again," he whispered in my ear sending shivers across my skin.

I pulled back so I could meet his gaze head on. I needed him to see how true the next few words I spoke were. "You won't," I said.

He furrowed his brow as he hesitated, and then he leaned forward to meet my lips.

Fireworks exploded through my body. This was what I was meant to do. Love Cade. He made me feel whole.

A home was no longer a big house with walls and over-priced furniture. It was the place I was with the people I loved. Eventually, the pain from my parent's divorce would lessen, and I would be able to see Dad's new house as a place I belonged in. And the moments I spent with Mom would make our house feel like home again.

But while my family life was a wreck, my life with Cade was perfect. For now, he would be my home.

When I pulled back, I studied him. "Thanks," I said.

He quirked an eyebrow. "For what?"

Heat raced to my cheeks. "Loving me."

He nodded and then his teasing smiled emerged. "That is so you. Forcing me to take charge and say something like that first."

I wiggled my eyebrows. "I don't know what you are talking about."

He pulled me closer. "I don't mind. I'll tell you first." He pressed his lips to my forehead before pulling back. "I love you, Chocolate Milk."

I snuggled into his chest. "I love you, too, Monster."

EPILOGUE

I pulled up to the courthouse a week later and turned off the engine. I glanced at my reflection in the mirror and straightened my ponytail. It was my first day, and I wanted to look presentable.

After I shoved my keys into my purse, I opened my door and stepped out.

I made my way up the steps of the courthouse and entered. Cade was standing next to the counter, chatting with an elderly woman on the other side. When he saw me, his smile lit up.

"Hey," he said, walking over to me and planting a kiss on my lips.

I giggled as I pulled back. "I'm not sure we are supposed to be doing this," I said, narrowing my eyes at him.

He shrugged. "I don't care."

When he leaned closer, I pressed my hand on his chest

and pushed him back. "I am *not* letting you get me in trouble again."

He wrinkled his nose as he pulled his most hurt expression. "That was *not* me."

"Cade Kelley, stop fraternizing with Penny," Ralph said as he walked into the foyer with a bunch of neon vests hanging from his arm.

"Porter? Gladia?" He called out. Two more people approached. "Welcome to community service," he said as he handed out the vests.

I took mine and slipped it on.

After had I talked to Cade, I contacted the judge. He was surprised that I actually wanted to pay my debt to society. Apparently, most people—well, everyone—tried to get out of doing community service. They didn't voluntarily offer themselves up for it. He had thought it was a joke at first, but I convinced him, and he let me join in.

Plus, it gave me more time to hang out with Cade. So it had its benefits.

After Ralph went over the rules, he turned and motioned for us to follow him.

Cade slipped his arm around my waist and pulled me close as we held back a little from the group. He nuzzled my hair. "I'm happy you are doing this with me. But you didn't have to," he said. His voice was gruff.

I turned toward him. "It's okay. It didn't feel right that you were the only one getting punished. I did something wrong, and I should do my part to fix that." I bit my lip as I turned to look at him. "Plus, seeing you in neon orange is doing something to my insides."

He raised his eyebrows. "Really?" Then he nodded. "Good to know."

I giggled as he leaned forward and pressed his lips to mine.

"Cade!" Ralph scolded.

He groaned and looked up. "Yeah?"

"Stop fraternizing with Penny."

Cade sighed and let me go. "This is going to be torture," he said under his breath.

I laughed. Torture or not, I was just happy to be next to him. He was my home, and I wasn't going anywhere.

I nodded toward Ralph and smiled at Cade. "Come on. We'll be fine."

He sighed. "Yeah. You're probably right. Besides, this will be harder for you because of your love for correctional colors," he said, waving toward his vest.

"True. But it's only two hours every week for"—I squinted as I tried to remember Judge Jones's stipulation —"fifty weeks." I shrugged. "No biggie."

Cade groaned. "I'm going to die," he said as he followed me out of the courthouse and over to the bus that was idling in the parking lot.

I laughed. "Well, I'll be here to resuscitate you."

He eyed me. "Promise?"

I nodded.

He sighed as he extended his hand out toward the stairs

of the bus. "After you."

As I passed by him, I grabbed his hand and gave it a squeeze. He responded with a smile and a squeeze back. As I sat in my designated seat, I glanced out the window. How strange this all was. A few weeks ago, if I had told myself that I would be sitting on a bus, headed for community service, I would have said I was crazy.

There was no way I would have ever done something like that for Cade. And now? He was my home. While my whole life tumbled down around me, he was there to support me. To love me.

So even though we sat on opposite sides of a bus headed to pick up litter from the side of the road, there was no place I would rather be.

I was home.

***

THANK you for reading Penelope and Cade's story! I hope you enjoyed breaking rule #2, you can't crush on your sworn enemy.

Up next is one of my most favorite tropes. Best friends to something more. And for Olivia, she's completely oblivious to the feelings of her best friend, Ethan.

When she comes with the great idea of auctioning him off so that she can win a chance of being with her ideal guy, Lachlan, it crushes Ethan.

Read exactly how they break the rules of love in their story:
Rule #3: You Can't Kiss your Best Friend

It was supposed to be a simple kiss. That was all. Whoops.
HERE!

JOIN THE NEWSLETTER

Want to learn about all of Anne-Marie Meyer's new releases
plus amazing deals from other authors?
Sign up for her newsletter today and get deals and
giveaways!
PLUS a free novella, Love Under Contract
TAKE ME TO MY FREE NOVELLA!
Also join her on these platforms:
Facebook
Instagram
anne-mariemeyer.com

Made in United States
Orlando, FL
18 July 2022

19902770R00129